Polis & Poltergeists

Alan Addison

ISBN: 978-1-4478-7834-6

Dedication

This book is dedicated to my friend Tom Attenburgh (Tracker) for his lifelong service to the youth of Newhaven and Leith and to the Scout Movement of Edinburgh and beyond.

Other Works of Fiction

Justified Sinner
Treaty of Union
Shaking Hands with a Tarantula
Finding Sophie
Working for Josh
Lullaby of the Soul

Non fiction
Using Scots in family literacy
Macnib's Legacy
Teachers notes, Scottish book trust

Glossary

Scots language is used by a few characters in the book. If this language is not one of yours, there is a Scots-English glossary at the end of the book. You can also find Scots language dictionaries on the world wide web.

CHAPTER ONE

Monday 8th June 2015

Bob was somewhat surprised when he tried to unlock the office door but found it unlocked. The first thing that came to mind was that JP Associates had been burgled. He pulled the handle down slowly and pushed the door gently.

'Morning Bob.' Tracey was sitting behind her desk.

'What in heaven's name…?'

'Now boss, you know how A feel about your blaspheming.'

He looked at the basket in the corner between her desk and the wall. 'Is that a dog? Where the bloody hell did that come from?'

Bertie sat bolt upright as if he had understood he was being addressed.

'Bertie is a present fae somebody.'

His eyes caught sight of something on the coat-stand. And what's with the deerstalker?'

'Harry bought me the hat tae go wie the dog Bertie is a bloodhound.'

The retired Detective Inspector shook his head and sat down hard by the coffee table. 'What are you doing in so early anyway?'

'A wanted tae surprise ye.'

'Well you've certainly done that?'

'A've been here most days at this time. A'm full time now, 9am till 5pm.'

'What? We can't afford that. And I don't remember discussing it with you.'

'You didnae need tae. Our HR manager agreed it.'

'Who? No, don't answer that. A little bird told me you were visiting Tod at the prison on Wednesday evenings.'

'Wrong, A'm not visiting Tod on Wednesday evening at the prison. We are teaching a literacy class thegither on Wednesday evenings. We only started last week. And anywie, he's not our HR manager, not for the moment at least.'

'Tracey, are you sure you're feeling alright?'

'Rebecca is our temporary HR manager, as well as our banker.'

'What! She didn't mention that.'

'Tod wrote to her and asked if she would step up in his absence. She jumped at it and offered me a full-time job, but that was only after she'd offered Josh Waterstone the admin job. He starts sometime in August.

'She never mentioned that either!'

'Oops.'

'And why are we going to need an admin assistant, we've got one, haven't we?'

'No, you've got a message lassie. Or should A say had one. As of today, A'm your assistant investigator on probation of course.'

Bob felt quite dizzy. 'So, Rebecca believes she has the right, as our funder, to promote you.'

'No, that was Tod. Rebecca only offered me full-time. But she's now agreed tae pay me Tod's salary until he returns - her Majesty is taking care of his keep for the present.'

'I really am being kept well and truly in the dark now eh. Is this some sort of feminist revenge on my masculinity?'

'No, you put yourself in the dark. I've not seen hide nor hair of you since Tod was arrested. Rebecca doesn't like mixing business wie pleasure so as you are staying there, she decided not tae discuss it wie ye. She said that once you came out of your sulk at losing your partner, the three of us can have weekly meetings in here. She wants to get you up tae speed and keep everyone in the loop. A just thought it best tae inform ye first.'

He was quiet for some time and looked as if he was going to explode, but didn't. 'Well partner, have we picked up any work in my absence?'

'A'll come tae that after A've been for the rolls – one wie sliced sausage and one wie bacon, brown sauce on both. You put the kettle on. A'm still your message lassie tae.'

Bob smiled for the first time that morning.

#

The two investigators sat quietly at the coffee table eating their rolls. Tracey was reading the Metro she'd picked up on the bus to work and Bob was pretending to read Greener Leith, the local rag.

She put down her newspaper. 'When are ye gonnae visit Tod?'

He kept hold of his magazine. 'Experience tells me that polis, retired or not, don't do prisoners much good by visiting them in jail. Anyway, from what I've heard he's being looked after well enough.' He dropped the magazine on the table.

'Looked after, what dae ye mean?'

'Your friend Mr McGuire.'

'You have your snitches Mr Witcher.'

He took the last bite of his bacon roll and continued with mouth half-full. 'What's the job?'

'Change the subject why don't ye. A Mr Molesworth, lawyer, was waiting at the door when I arrived this morning.'

'And?'

'He's having some sort of trouble with anti-social behaviour.'

'That's a job for the Council, or Police Scotland, if it's bad enough.'

'Oh it's bad, but A dinnae think the Council, or the polis, would be interested.'

'Why not?'

'It's a poltergeist that's causing the problem.' At the sound of the word "poltergeist" Bertie yelped and jumped from his basket.

Bob, having just taken a large sip of his tea, spat it all over Greener Leith. 'A poltergeist!'

'That's right. The man is being haunted. He was in a terrible state. I told him A'd speak to you about it and reassured him we would get on the case and get to the bottom of it for him.'

'Are you sure you are alright Tracey?'

'Never felt better. Anyway, he's left us his keys and we are going there tonight at midnight. Last night, just after midnight, he was wakened by a light shining under his bedroom door and could see a shadow moving back and forward in the hall outside. When he turned to wake his Doberman, which sleeps in a basket by his bed, the dog was standing upright and was shaking uncontrollably. The man swore it's hair was standing on end.'

'And you believed him?'

'Of course, A believed him. He's a lawyer and has a successful law company in Queen Charlotte Street. Charles Molesworth Solicitors. He lives in the two floors about the office. He is not the type of man to make this up. He's a wreck!'

'I've heard of a Charles Molesworth. If it's the same one, he's an ambulance chaser, you know the lawyers who will get you compensation if you have been injured in any way. He was in all the newspapers a while back. He encouraged an individual to take out a case against the Fishermens Union, something about an accident in the docks. The individual in question scored a large, but undisclosed sum of money.' Bob thought for a moment. 'I still don't understand why we have to meet at midnight?'

'Cause it's June and it won't be dark till then.'

They'd agreed to meet outside the police station in Queen Charlotte Street at 11.45pm. Bob leaned on the railings outside the station speaking to a police constable when Tracey drew up in a taxi. The policeman took his cue and walked into the building as Bob walked towards the cab.

'I thought Harry was bringing you?'

'Dinnae mention Harry tae me. He was supposed tae be bringing me but he and his boss had things to discuss after work and went tae some New Town wine bar. He was over the limit to drive when he got hame.'

'Always said he was a bad lot that Harry Cowan.'

'Aye, well if he keeps snuggling up tae Mrs Spale he'll get mair than the jail fae me.' Tracey had never gotten over Bob arresting her man years before.

'Well are we going to get this over with. That young constable was wondering what I was doing here at this time of night.'

'What did you tell him?'

'That I was taking my secretary for a wee late-night drinkie.'

'Ye what!'

'That's why he scuttled off when you arrived.'

'You should be so lucky Bob James. And A'm not your secretary, not any longer!'

'Well super-sleuth, we'd better get a move on or the ghosties and ghouls will be away to their beds. By the way, where's Bertie?'

'A was worried he'd attack the Doberman so A left him wie Casanova.'

They headed eastwards along Queen Charlotte Street. 'So where is this haunted house exactly?'

'It's only a fifty yards fae here, on the left.'

'We better get a move on then or we'll miss the witching hour.'

#

As the two investigators climbed the eight steps to the door they saw the brightly polished brass plaque on the wall announcing that this was the premises of a solicitor. Tracey took the bunch of keys from her handbag while Bob stood behind her checking for on-lookers while shaking his head in disbelief. Tracey waited for the creak as she pushed the door, but none came.

The hallway was completely dark. Bob took out his mobile phone and shone the torch on a notice board that held some pictures of houses for sale. The rest of the space was taken up by achievement certificates and rules and regulations, giving the idea that one was in the hands of an honest lawyer. 'And I don't think,' whispered Bob as he shone his torch away from the board towards the staircase.

As they stepped lightly up the stairs they heard a ticking sound behind them. Bob leaned over the banister and looked down. The sound was coming from a corner in the dark stairwell. 'I hope that's not a cuckoo clock,' whispered Bob, 'it might frighten the ghosts.'

'Cut the comedy and be quiet, A'm trying tae concentrate.'

He could see that Tracey was on edge, though not as much as himself.

When they reached the first floor all the room doors were closed. They both expected to hear Molesworth's Doberman burst into life but there was no sound. Bob put his hand into the inside pocket of his jacket and wrapped his fingers around the police extendable baton.

'Is that a gun ye've got in there Clint?'

'Very funny.'

'A little bird told me you've a liking for a hand-gun.'

'And what little bird would that be, as if I didn't know.'

Both became conscious that they'd lowered their voices till they could hardly hear each other.

'So what now,' asked Bob.

Just then they heard a whimper from behind a door at the end of the corridor. Bob put his hand on Tracey's shoulder and moved her aside. He was at the door in seconds and turning the handle; his baton held tightly in his other hand. He pushed the door gently.

Tracey came into the room to find him frozen to the spot. He was staring along the torch beam to the dog cowering in its basket. Then he moved the beam to the bed. The solicitor was lying on top of the bedcovers. He had a dressing gown on top of his clothes and a large kitchen knife in his hand. There was no sign of any blood but a terrible stench hung over the room.

Bob walked over to the corpse to check for signs of life but knew, even before doing so, that he was well, and truly dead. His pallor was the greyest Bob had ever seen on a corpse, and he'd seen a few of those. He saw that a trickle of blood had dried on the man's lip. He'd heard of people's hair standing on end but this man's silver grey made a mockery of that; they spiked straight out from his scalp ridged as a hedgehog's spines.

'He certainly looks like he's died of fright,' whispered Tracey, looking around warily for the cause of the apparition. 'What are we gaun tae dae now? We'll need tae get the polis.'

'I am the polis.'

'You were the polis. We're private investigators, remember.'

'Polis or not, I can tell you what we're going to do now. We are getting out of here, sharpish.'

'Are we gaun tae the cop shop along the street?'

'Not on your life. When we leave here you are going to the nearest phone box and phoning them. Tell them you were passing and thought you heard weird noises coming from the house.'

'Is that it? We cannae just leave the poor man lying here.'

'Just watch me. Do you think for one minute that I am going to try to explain to some jumped up inspector that Bob James was on a ghost hunt? No, my dear Watson, not on your life. Our client isn't going anywhere, is he. Now let's get those handles wiped.

CHAPTER TWO

Tuesday 9th June

'I still can't believe you did that.'

'Rebecca, give it a rest. I told you when I got in but you've kept me up half the night trying to explain myself. We left the scene and Tracey called 999 and said she'd been walking past Molesworth's house and heard noises. She said she could not give her name as she did not want her estranged husband to find out that she was out at that time of night.'

Rebecca was preparing breakfast while questioning Bob. 'Tracey and Harry have not split up, have they?'

'No, it was a ruse, but they soon will if he continues playing the field with Mrs Spale.'

She opened the oven and put the hot croissants in a basket and placed it on the table. 'I know about that, that's why I asked.' She sat down. 'So, you left Molesworth lying dead and asked Tracey to phone the police?'

'That is exactly what I did. It's a matter for the police now and absolutely nothing to do with JP Associates.'

'But Mr Molesworth was already our client.' Just as she said this her daughter Sophie walked sleepily into the kitchen. 'Good morning Bobby. Hi Mum.' She took a seat beside Bob. 'Who is Mr Molesworth?'

'I'm afraid it's who was Mr Molesworth, Sophie. He was a somewhat infamous lawyer, what we call an ambulance chaser.'

'I've heard of them.'

‘Are you two going to eat breakfast or are you going to talk all morning?’ interjected Rebecca.

‘Mummy, did I hear you say that Mr Molesworth was our client?’

‘Yes dear, I did, but Bobby decided to give our case to the police.’

‘Why did you do that Bobby?’

‘It’s a long story Sophie.’

‘What he is trying to say Sophie, is that he didn’t want anything to do with the case as Mr Molesworth had complained of being haunted and ghosts are obviously not on Bobby’s to do list. Isn’t that right Bobby.’

He was about to answer, in no uncertain terms, when his mobile rang. ‘Bob, did you hear about that solicitor, Charles Molesworth. He was found dead in the early hours of the morning and he looked as if he’d been frightened to death.’ It was DI Sandra Laing.

Fuck, thought Bob. ‘Mr Molesworth? Are you on that case Sandra?’

‘Yep. The powers that be thought it best if I rejoined the present day. I’m with the murder squad now. DS Mackay is working with me. The Cold Case Squad has a new leader and Margaret is his underling.’ There was silence for a moment before she continued. ‘You knew Molesworth, didn’t you?’

Bob stood, took a large sip of his coffee, and walked to the door. ‘Only from what I read in the papers regarding the case with the Fishermens Union. He wasn’t the type you’d want against you in a court of law, particularly a libel action. Do you remember the Fishermens Union case? He did them over, well and truly over.’

‘Aye, and nearly put the charity down the proverbial That’s what I heard anyway.’

‘I take it that’s not why you’re phoning, is it?’

'No, I just thought I'd run it past you while you were on the phone. It's about your central heating boiler, it's not working and I had to have a cold shower this morning.'

'That will not do you any harm Sandra. I'm getting the cold shoulder this morning.'

'Mm. Do you want me to phone an engineer or do you have one you use?'

'Just leave the engineer to me, I'll get right on to it.' Bob ended the call, walked back into the kitchen and sat down. 'That was Sandra, my central heating boiler's acting up. I'll have to phone the engineer.'

'So Sandra has been given the Molesworth case?'

'Listen, I have to go back to Portobello and wait for the engineer.'

'But you've not made an appointment as yet.'

Bob stood again, leaned over and gave Sophie and peck on the cheek. She in turn threw her mother a look of disdain that said she was treading on dangerous territory and if not careful, he may not return from his house in Portobello.

#

Harry had set the breakfast table for Tracey as he did every morning before heading to work, but when she appeared she was not in the mood for conversation.

'You were in late last night,' said Harry as he poured the tea.

'So were you.'

'It was after two o'clock in the morning when you got in.'

She sipped her tea but made no effort to reach for the rack of toast.

'It's your favourite. Seeded wholemeal lightly done.'

'Smashing.'

'Tracey, A'm sorry about last night. Mrs Spale wanted to talk to me about investors left over from the Gormand case. They're still with the company and probably benefactors of the tontine. She's really worried they might defraud the company.'

She took the bait. 'And what did she want to talk to you for? What dae you ken about finance?'

'Well it wisnae about finance really. A'd told her about Hacker Hanson a while back and she wanted tae ken aw about him and whether we could enlist his help in tracking down the funds.'

'Mm.'

'That's the truth. A messaged Hacker when you were out last night and he's up for it.'

'A think you're up for it tae Harry Cowan and A dinnae ken what tae believe.'

'You've got Mrs Spale aw wrong hen. She's really nice, and she likes you.'

'She hardly kens me.'

Harry realised he was getting nowhere. Chr…is that the time.' He left the table much as Bob had left Rebecca's.

The second she heard the front door close Tracey unplugged her phone she'd left charging on the kitchen worktop overnight.

The reply came within seconds. **'Of course we can meet this morning Tracey. I'll see you in the office at ten.'** Callum put his phone back into his old leather briefcase beside his bible and wondered what JP Associates where up to now that they'd need a minister.

#

As Bob drew up outside his Georgian Terraced flat he saw that the engineer's van was parked two doors along. He was doubly surprised to see DI Sandra Laing's car parked behind it.

'I'll have to keep you on as a lodger Sandra. You didn't have to wait for Craig.'

The engineer had his back to Bob and his head buried in the boiler. 'Morning Bob, he mumbled. 'I was passing when I got your call and came straight here.'

'And as I'm the one going without a hot shower, I thought it prudent to let Craig fix the boiler before I headed off. I'll be going back to Molesworth's. Do you want to come along?'

'Me? No, I'll wait for Craig to finish up.'

'It's okay,' answered Craig, squinting over his shoulder. 'I'll lock up and put the keys through the letterbox. I'll email you the bill.'

'There were one or two things I wanted to talk through with you about the heating system.'

'Dinnae worry about that, I'll check the whole system before I go.'

'Do I detect a slight reticence Mr James,' said Sandra.

'Well, I'm no longer your consultant.'

'Oh, I see, in the cream-puff. Your help with this case would be much appreciated, and I'm sure that can be reciprocated. Nothing like having a DI as friend when one runs a detective agency.'

Bob turned to the engineer. 'Thanks Craig, I'll leave the keys on the shelf at the door.'

#

On their way to Queen Charlotte Street Sandra filled Bob in regarding what they'd found at Molesworth's house. The young constable who was sent to investigate the anonymous call, swore he saw a figure at the first-floor window prior to entering the house. The front door was unlocked and the only sound was a clock ticking behind the staircase. She described the condition he'd found the body in, much as Bob had witnessed it earlier. Apparently when the constable returned to the station to report it he looked as if he'd seen a ghost.

'Are you alright Bob?'

'Aye.'

'You look as if you've seen one too. Is everything alright with you and Rebecca?'

'Aye, we have our moments, that's all.'

'Listen if you want to move back to your place I can find somewhere else.'

'Sandra, there's no way I could see you on the street. You'll just have to settle in as my room-mate; I'm sure we could come to some arrangement.'

'Aye right Bob James, not on your life!'

#

Callum spotted Bertie the bloodhound the second he opened the door to JP Associates office. He noticed the deerstalker on the coat stand too and smiled.

'Tod gave it tae me. The dog, not the hat.'

'Mm. What's his name?'

'Bertie. He gave him tae me just before he was arrested.'

'How are you coping without him Tracey?'

'A'm missing him.'

'Tod Peterson's a good man, murder conviction or not.'

'He was working for the Security Services.'

'I've heard much the same myself. How is Valerie coping?

'We've not seen hide nor hair of her since he went to jail. She's probably thrown herself intae her work. She a good artist and I bet she's a good teacher as well.'

'I've got one or two of her paintings.'

'Aye, Tod told me.'

'Is that all he told you?'

'There's nothing else tae tell, is there?'

'No, I just wondered. Anyway, what did you want to speak to me about?'

'I'll put the kettle on. A got some mini-doughnuts on the way in.'

Callum followed her into the kitchen. 'How's Harry?'

'Same as ever. Ye ken Harry.'

'I do.'

They returned to the front office and sat at the coffee table. Callum waited.

'Dae you believe in spirits?'

'Only two. Our Lord's and our uisge beatha.'

'Mm.'

'Why do you ask?'

'A think Bob and I might have stumbled upon another kind in the early hours of this morning.'

'Not the kind that go bump in the night.'

After she had told Callum the tale, and sworn him to secrecy, he leaned back against his chair. 'A Mr Molesworth you say?'

'Aye.'

'I know of him. I was pastor to the seamen when he took the Fishermens Union to court for libel. In fact, I tried to talk him out of it, but he was for none of that. He won his case of course and the charity nearly collapsed.'

'Aye Bob told me that.'

'But I know of another Mr Molesworth.'

'Who's that?'

'A Mr Molesworth whose case dates back to the 1830s. He inhabited a rented property in the newly built area of Trinity. He claimed he was being haunted and it was all caused by his landlord who lived in the adjoining house. What a coincidence that your Mr Molesworth is suffering the same fate.'

'Was suffering the same fate, he's dead remember.'

'Oh aye. Why did Bob want to leave the scene? That's not like him, at all.'

‘I think he was worried about his reputation. He’s always been seen as a straight down the middle kind of person, everything in black and white, and involvement in an investigation involving poltergeists and ghost was probably too much for him.’

‘But to leave the scene of a possible crime? No, I don’t believe it, not Bob James.’

‘Well that’s what he said. He didn’t want to explain to the police that he was on a ghost hunt. But that aside, what do you believe about creatures that go bump in the night?’

‘I used to read a lot of Dennis Wheatley when I was young. The Devil Rides Out and such like.’

‘Who?’

‘Dennis Wheatley. He wrote novels about the occult; I loved his Duke De Richleau character. He was the devil’s antithesis and the hero of some of Wheatley’s novels. Richleau travelled on what the writer called the astral plain, a sort of spiritual global highway.’

‘You surprise me Minister.’

‘That was well before I took the cloth you understand.’

‘So what do you believe now?’

‘I haven’t thought much about it in recent years, though it may help quantify my feelings on the subject if I told you I would never get involved in a séance or a Ouija board. That’s just two examples of course.’

‘Why would you not?’

‘That story is for another day I’m afraid.’ Callum, stood to go.

‘You’ve not finished your tea. Would you agree tae exorcise an evil spirit if ye were asked?’

He didn’t answer.

#

As he was leaving the office, Sandra and Bob were entering Molesworth’s house. Much to Bob’s chagrin, the young constable who he'd seen outside the station just after midnight was standing by the door.

Bob put his finger to his lips to indicate that the young man should say nothing of their meeting. The young man winked in return.

'Am I missing something here?' asked Sandra, looking from one to the other.

'Walter's the son of my second-cousin Mary,' said Bob.

'What a small world.'

'That's Leith for you,' he answered, following her into the premises.

Sandra walked towards the staircase, leaving her ex-boss rooted to the spot inside the front door. The clock was still ticking, louder than ever.

'Well come on you big bugger, we've not got all morning. What are you looking at anyway?'

'Just checking the notice board.'

'Well get a move on!' She began climbing the stairs.

Bob followed. 'Is the body still here?'

'No, it'll be off to the pathologists by now.'

'So what am I doing here exactly?'

'There something I want you to see. Something that has me intrigued.'

When they reached the first landing he expected her to go straight to the bedroom but she stopped and opened a narrow panelled door to their left and disappeared inside. Bob followed and was surprised to see her climb a narrow spiral staircase.

'This leads to the attic.'

Bob had to stoop to avoid the low ceiling.

'Wait till you set your eyes on this little surprise.' She opened another small door, causing cobwebs to float gently onto Bob's shoulders.

As he followed her in, still bent double, he walked straight into her back. He was staring past her to the chalk drawing on the floor. 'What in Heaven's name is that?' he almost shouted.

'It's an occult pentagram. That horny old goat in the centre represents Old Nick. It looks like our Mr Molesworth was into black magic.' When she turned Bob wasn't there and all she could hear was his heavy footsteps tread the creaking boards on the way down. She followed him but by the time she got to the first floor he had gone into the bathroom. 'Are you alright Bob?'

'Aye, I'll only be a minute. It must have been something I ate. My tummy's giving me gip.'

#

By the time Bob arrived at the office Tracey had just returned from Greggs with her lunch. 'Am I smelling hot sausage roll?' he asked.

'Aye. And you're right in your use of the singular, A've only got one.'

'Did you not get me anything?'

'And how was A supposed tae know when you'd be in, or if you'd be in?'

'You'll understand once I've told you where I've been. I'll just nip round and get my lunch. I'll be back in two ticks.'

'Dinnae bother, A bought two, and a pie.'

'Tracey, you really are a mind reader. Which is just as well, it looks like we are going to need one.'

'Gies a minute, A'll put the kettle on then you can tell me all about it.'

Supping their tea and trying not to spill the crumbs of the day's fayre on the table and carpet, Bob told her about his return visit to Molesworth's.

'Tracey nearly spat out a mouthful of tea.' 'Why did ye agree tae go back? Did ye get a pang of conscience?'

'No, Sandra Laing decided she needed my input. She's in charge of the investigation. She's with the murder squad now.'

'A ken that. She was in here a few days ago, before you decided to came back to work.'

'And you decided not to tell me? Maybe Tod was right and there's not enough sharing of information around here.'

'Maybe he was. Does she know we were there in the early hours of this morning?'

'She knows nothing about our involvement. I was back at my place this morning to meet my heating engineer and Sandra was just leaving to go back to Molesworth's and asked me to go with her.'

'Dae ye think she suspects we're involved? She's no daft.'

'No, she's just flummoxed with this case and not sure where to turn.'

'Did ye find out anything else when ye were at the lawyers?'

'Aye.' Bob suddenly went very quiet.

'Is everything awright?'

'We found a pentagram.'

'A what?'

'A star shape drawing on the floor of the attic. There was an image of a horned goat in the centre with esoteric symbols all around it.'

'A've seen that on programmes on the tellie; it's black magic.'

'Aye.'

CHAPTER THREE

Saturday 13th June

'Well this is a surprise.'

'I'm sorry I've not been to see you before now. You're looking well.'

'It's the prison diet. I wish I could say the same for you; you're not looking too good. Have I caused that by ending up here?'

'Well, I must admit, it's kept me on my toes. I've lost the consultancy work with Police Scotland.'

'Does that mean JP Associates closing?'

'No, Rebecca has upped the funding due to my loss of earnings.' I can still make do on my police pension. Talking about police, Sandra has been moved to the murder squad and Margaret Whalen, not your favourite policewoman by all accounts, has a new DI on the Cauld Case Squad.

'DC Whalen always thought you'd pull her partner Sandra back from the dark side and here she is living in your house.'

Bob smiled. 'Nowt funnier than folk. How are things in here?'

'Lovely.'

'A little bird tells me that you're being well looked after by a certain inmate who for the sake of modesty shall remain nameless.'

'Does that little bird's name begin with the letter T by any chance? And that's not T for Tweet.'

Bob's smile grew wider. 'She says I was wrong and your guardian angel definitely has turned over a new leaf. What's your take on it?'

'She's right.' Tod leaned back in his chair. 'Well, are you going to tell me why you've come to see me?'

He looked around once more before telling his friend and business partner the whole story then waited for an answer.

'It strikes me,' answered Tod, after some minutes, 'that there are two things at play here. One, ghosts do exist, you can take my word on that, I've one in my cell with me every night. The other is that you have met your nemesis.'

'What do you mean?'

'The great and good Detective Inspector Bob James, upright and fearless has met his match.'

'Are you taking the piss?'

'No. Do you not remember telling me when we were still at school that you were dead scared, was how you put it, of ghosts?' Apparently, your parents used to hang their coats on the back of your bedroom door and when they closed the door once you were in bed the coats used to move and wander about the room. Your parents wouldn't listen to you when you complained. Am I right?'

Bob was about to argue then changed his mind. 'Aye. Do you remember telling me how your older siblings consistently ribbed you about you being a mistake? So, if I were you I wouldn't share that information about my being frightened of ghosts.'

'I see, you are still really touchy about it. I wouldn't tell anyone about your phobias, would I?'

Bob could almost see the horns under his friend's hair, reminding him that the word Tod can mean Devil in Scots. 'Anyway, enough of that. What are we going to do about Molesworth?'

‘So, the “royal we” finds its way into prisons too. It’s for the police to decide what to do about Molesworth, is it not?’

‘Yes it is. But since when did JP Associates let a wee thing like the police, or fear of spirits, or its leading light serving a jail sentence stand in its way?’

‘What do you think we could achieve that the police couldn’t?’

‘Well obviously there is something going on that has nothing to do with the Devil or any other evil spirit. Someone was out to get that lawyer and we need to find that someone or our reputation might suffer?’

‘Reputation, that’s a laugh. Tracey told me Molesworth was responsible for a libel claim that all but bankrupted the Fishermens Union in Leith. He’s bound to have made some enemies there. But there may be others. He was an ambulance chaser and many could have suffered from that.’

‘I’m not sure when it was that he took that title. It might have been after the Fishermens Union case?’

‘That’s it then, you’ll have to visit the Fishermens Union.’

‘Right boss. Could you organise the relevant expenses and planning at your end?’

‘I’d love to, if I was anything other than a silent partner, for the moment anyway.’

Bob stood. ‘Aye so you are. I’d better be off partner.’ He looked down at Tod. ‘Were you really working for MI5?’

‘Tod stood and looked across the table at his lifelong friend. ‘Whatever gave you that idea?’

CHAPTER FOUR

Monday 15th June

'What time is our meeting?'

'Our meeting?

'The meeting with the Fishermens Union.' Rebecca was looking into her dressing room mirror and brushing her long red hair as Bob leaned on the door frame to her bedroom. She could see his dour reflection in the glass and resisted a reply.

'I've not phoned them yet, let alone have a meeting with them. And anyway, since the powers that be decided that Tracey was to be my full-time partner in JP Associates I think it's only fair for her to be at that meeting, don't you?'

The smile left Rebecca's lips as fast as it had appeared. 'Always one to have the last word Bobby.'

Appearing to pay no attention, he took his mobile phone from his trouser pocket. 'Is that you Tracey?'

'Aye, who else dae ye think it wid be? And what are ye daen phoning at this time. A've not even had ma breakfast.'

'When you get to the office could you phone the Fishermens Union in Constitution Street, the number will be on their website. Make an appointment for you and I. Oh and Tracey, make it today if possible.'

Tracey knew her boss well enough to know that something was playing out at Gamekeepers Road. *'What time will you be in?'*

'As soon as I can get away.'

She heard the unspoken end of his sentence "from here" loud and clear.

#

Both investigators plus Bertie arrived at the office spot on nine. Bertie looked pleased with himself, Tracey did not.

'Harry playing up again,' said Bob as she unlocked the door.

'No, it's you.' She headed straight for the kitchen and the kettle.

Bob followed her. 'What have I done now?'

'What have you not done? You do realise that Rebecca funds our work and since you've lost your consultancy wie Police Scotland she is our only hope of survival. Without her funding we are down the toilet.'

He leaned both hands on the kitchen worktop. 'I'd no choice, she wanted to take your place at the Fishermens Union meeting. I couldn't have that now, could I?'

'Is that the truth?'

'It sure is. She might be our funder but you are an investigator now and we can't have her stepping on your toes, can we?'

She wasn't sure whether to smile or cry. If Rebecca chose she could pull the funding and there would be no JP Associates to go to any meeting. She smiled nevertheless.

'When you've made the coffee you could give the Fishermens Union a phone.'

'Right boss!'

'In your own time of course.'

Bob took his mug into the main office, sat down at the coffee table and watched as Tracey took to her swivel chair behind her desk and phoned the Fishermens Union.

'Yes that's right. We are investigating the death of one Mr Charles Molesworth, solicitor. We believe your charity was known to him.'

It was Bob's turn to smile.

‘Of course I can hold on.’ They waited. ‘Yes, 11am would be perfect.’ She put down the phone. ‘Eleven o’clock at their offices on Constitution Street.’

‘I heard. I see you didn’t mention we were private investigators so they’d think we’re the police. Your friend and mine has taught you well.’

She ignored that. ‘Well dinnae just sit there ogling me working. Have you nothing tae keep ye occupied till then?’

‘As a matter of fact I do.’ He took out his phone. ‘Is that you Craig?’

‘It is Bob.’

You’ve not sent me the bill for the job, which I’ve got to say, has worked a treat. My lodger’s delighted.’

‘Aye, she came back before I left. I was there until teatime.’

‘You were what?’

‘Aye.’

‘That’ll cost me an arm and a leg!’

‘It’s not that bad. Are ye sitting down?’

Bob cut the line.

‘I meant have ye nothing tae keep ye occupied that might resemble investigative work,’ interrupted Tracey.

‘It was work,’ answered Bob. The case of the rip-off heating engineer!’

#

The offices of the Fishermens Union reminded Bob of Croan’s trawler offices in Granton. When he was a youngster he’d be sent there to pick up the pay his Dad had earned landing fish on the harbour. The Fishermens Union office even had the corrugated glass sliding panel separating the receptionist from the public.

The panel slid aside once they’d entered the small lobby. ‘Can I help you?’

'We're here about the Molesworth case,' answered Bob. As he'd hoped, they were not asked for identification.

'It's the second door on the right.' The mention of Molesworth's name put a somewhat distasteful look on the receptionist's face.

Bob knocked.

'Come in.'

An elderly gent was sitting behind an ancient mahogany desk. He stood as they entered and extended his large hand. 'Willie Dewar, ex trawler skipper and director of this weary band.'

'Pleased to meet you Willie. Bob James and this is Tracey Cowan.'

'Hi Tracey. Did you not bring a Greggs with you?' The Union man smiled broadly. 'Aye, I know who you are and who you work for. It's amazing what one picks up in the queue at Greggs.' He turned to Bob. 'And you'll be her boss in JP Associates. I was sorry to hear about your partner, a terrible thing that. Please take a seat.

Bob felt the urge to tell Willie Dewar about Tod's involvement with MI5 but chose to keep his council. 'Aye it was.' They sat down.

'So our Mr Molesworth has met his end. I cannae say I'm sorry to be honest.'

'Have you had any dealing with him since the court case?'

'So you know about that. We've only had the occasional reminder to make sure our monthly cheque was in the post.'

'Why else would we be here,' answered Bob. 'You didn't pay the costs in a oner after the verdict?'

'We couldn't; it would have bankrupted us. Fortunately, the judge had some sympathy and allowed us to pay the claim and costs monthly. We're still on the brink mind you and had to get rid of most of our paid staff. Gladys who you met at reception is the only one remaining.'

'How did you take that, your charity failing?'

'Well I wasn't laughing all the way to the bank, that's for sure. And some believed that we were to blame for Brian's accident so in their eyes we'd already failed.'

'Brian, he was the one who fell into the water between two boats and was crushed, is that correct?'

'Yes.'

'From what we heard he was somewhat the worse for wear with the drink.'

'That's right, Brian had a liking for the bottle.'

'He was involved with your charity because of his drinking?'

'We were trying to help him come off the hard stuff. That was why we gave him the task of delivering a letter to one of the skippers of the boats that he ended up falling between. We wanted to give him some responsibility. We couldn't foresee that Brian would hit every pub between here and the docks before going in the water. And the rest is history. Two and a half million pounds plus costs.'

'Do you have any members or staff who might take the law intae their own hands to get revenge on Molesworth?' asked Tracey.

'We've members who are more than capable of doing as you suggest, they were trawlermen remember, but I would think it highly unlikely they would go that far. And violence certainly wouldn't have been sanctioned by the Fishermens Union. So Molesworth was murdered then?'

'We're still not sure. It could be natural causes,' answered Bob

'Or unnatural causes,' added Tracey.

'Pardon? Was there something unnatural about his death?'

‘We’d better be going Tracey; we’ve taken up enough of Mr Dewar’s time,’ said Bob, standing.

Tracey stood and lifted her bag from the floor. ‘Thank you for agreeing seeing us Mr Dewar. She handed him a business card. ‘Please phone if there is anything you can tell us that may help.

#

As they walked up Constitution Street Tracey asked Bob if he thought Willie Dewar capable of orchestrating the death of Molesworth. Bob said he wasn’t convinced, but that was only until she explained that it was possible that the debt owed to Molesworth might be cancelled on his death.’

‘But that would mean that Brian Bain was also in danger. You’re turning out to be more of a detective than meets the eye Marlow.’

‘And you’re at the ham Bob James.’

Just as she said this Bob’s mobile rang. ‘Sandra, what can I do for you?’

‘You can stop interfering in a police investigation!’

He put his finger over the mike and looked at Tracey. ‘Oops.’

‘I thought you wanted me involved?’

‘I wanted a second opinion, not a team of gumshoes treading all over my case!’

‘How’s the heating system? Are you getting that hot shower now?’

‘And don’t try to sweet talk me!’

‘How do you know we’ve just left the Fishermens Union? No, don’t answer that. Queen Charlotte Street canaries been singing again?’

‘JP Associates interfering in the Molesworth case is not on Bob. Are you in the office?’

‘No, we’re about to take Bertie for his afternoon stroll around Leith Links.’ He winked at Tracey.

‘Well when you’ve done walking the dog let me know and I’ll be straight round.’ She hung up.

He put his mobile back in his pocket. ‘It would seem that our Willie Dewar is not the nice friendly ex-skipper we thought. He’s gone and phoned the polis the second we left and reported our visit.’

Bertie was pleased to see them when they entered the office. He took his lead in his mouth and brought it to Tracey.

‘I bet you wish Harry was as attentive as that,’ said Bob, bending to clap the dog.

‘Harry’s lead is about tae tighten, eh Bertie,’ replied Tracey.

#

It was a lovely June afternoon as the pair and dog walked together through the park.

‘Tod’s looking well.’

‘Have you been tae see him? Ye kept that one quiet.’

‘Aye like you kept quiet about the changes in the office.’

‘Mm.’

Bertie enjoyed his daily walks around the Links and was running wildly chasing and being chased by much bigger dogs.

Bob and Tracey took to a bench with a view east across the park. ‘Is Tod doing alright?’ asked Bob.

‘A think so. He seems tae enjoy the literacy classes.’

‘He had a great reputation when he worked in North Telford; got local and national awards for his work.’

‘He was brilliant wie me and the bairns at Granton School. A couldnae read or write so A couldnae help the bairns wie their homework, but he was able tae quell aw ma fears and get me tae college.’

‘Aye he’s a clever bloke.’ Bob stared across the park at the Leith lunchtime scene. Dog walkers having meetings, builders in white helmets eating carry-outs, school kids, eating carry-outs. Seagulls threatening them all. 'Don't cook, just eat,' said Bob.'

'What?'

'Nothing. Do you think Tod really was working for MI5? Has he mentioned it to you?'

'He hasn't said one word about it, but it is possible, he did go tae Cambridge Uni. Gies a minute, A'm just gaun tae get Bertie, he's too near that road.'

Bob watched as she headed towards the road that divides the park in two. She grabbed Bertie by the collar and hooked his lead on. A man was hoisting himself into a black van only yards from her.

She returned to the bench with the dog. 'Did ye see the joker get intae that van?'

'Aye, what of it?'

'A think he was gonnae lift Bertie.'

'Dogs like Bertie are worth a small fortune. Stay there.' Bob was up on his feet and moving at pace across the grass. As he got near the van it revved up and drove off. The windows were blackened, preventing him from seeing who was inside.

'Well that racing start tells me that whoever he was, he was up to no good.'

'A've seen vans like that before.'

'Where?'

'At the Western General Hospital. That's the type of van they take the dead bodies away in at night.'

Bob didn't answer but suddenly felt chill. 'We better be getting back, Sandra will be wanting to speak with us.'

#

They returned to Great Junction Street and the office via the Kirkgate. As they past Jake's bench Tracey hesitated. 'A really miss him.'

'Funnily enough, so do I.'

'He did a lot for JP Associates.'

'Especially with his collecting tin research. He kept the polis in a job too when he was younger.'

Tracey laughed out loud at the memory of Jake with Tod and then with Mark doing his own form of investigation through collecting monies under false pretences. In each case he got JP the information it needed but his style almost led to their arrest.

'No wonder you're laughing,' said Bob, as he turned towards the office.

'A widnae be in too much of a hurry if A were you. Look what's waiting for ye.'

He immediately saw what she was referring too. 'Shit.'

'Aye, and you are right in it.'

'Don't you mean we?'

'Oh here we go again the royal we; JP Associates answer to everything. In other places it might be called passing the buck.'

As they approached Bob could see the steam coming from Sandra's ears. 'Alright Sandra?'

She didn't answer but waited for Tracey to unlock the door then waited until they were well inside the office and the door was firmly closed. 'For fuck's sake Bob, what did you think you were doing going to see the Fishermens Union? You don't work for us anymore!'

'That's not what you said the other day when you asked me to accompany you to Molesworth's house.'

'That was just to get your take on it, it didn't give you carte blanch to stamp your brogues all over the case. It now looks like we could be dealing with a murder here and the last thing I need after that fiasco finding Josh is you sticking your big fucking neb in again! If the Super finds out that JP Associates has involved itself in this case I could lose my job! For fuck sake Bob, I'm only just back after that last suspension the one I have you to thank for!'

'Sandra, you'll need to calm down. Tracey, go and make the Inspector a fruit tea.'

'A fucking fruit tea?'

'Mm. If my memory serves me well Sandra, wasn't that suspension your own fault? The way that you and your underling dealt with that visit to Gormand and Spale left much to be desired. That's what got you suspended, not me.'

'That's true Sandra.' Tracey handed her a mug of tea. 'It's lemon and ginger.'

'Well excuse me for asking Tracey, but what has any of this to do with you?'

'A'm a junior partner in this agency and it's ma place to protect our reputation even if that threat is coming fae the polis.' A cannae have you spreading false information about JP Associates.'

Sandra sat down hard by the coffee table, took a sip of her tea and grimaced.

'I think you'd better get DI Laing a proper cuppa, don't you Tracey?'

By the time she returned with the fresh coffees and the bag of mini-doughnuts the Detective Inspector had calmed, but only slightly. 'Bob, when you visited Molesworth's with me did you notice the large ornate pottery jug on the dressing table in his bedroom?'

Bob thought for a moment. 'Nope, I wasn't in his bedroom remember. We went straight upstairs to the attic.' He couldn't work out whether Sandra was trying to catch him out as having been at the scene of crime earlier.

'Oh silly me, of course you weren't.'

'Was there something in the jug?' asked Tracey.

‘Well it isn’t a jug in the straight sense of the word, it’s an urn. It was full of ashes but was no ashtray either. It’s been tested by forensics and they were the ashes of more than one human being. Molesworth either had a lot of deceased relations or he was collecting macabre mementos. The dig team are in the courtyard of the place now and will be turning their talents to the front garden once they’ve completed their search out the back. Just as well the Leith Gala finished on Saturday or we would have had to build a viewing platform.’

‘I’ll refill the kettle,’ said Bob, before disappearing into the kitchen.

‘Is he alright?’ asked Sandra.

‘A’m not sure. He has been acting strangely recently. A just put that down tae his somewhat tempestuous relationship wie Rebecca.’

‘Rebecca’s alright, isn’t she?’

‘Aye but it’s not a match made in Heaven. Bob is Granton born and bred and she is pure Cramond, wie a property portfolio tae match.’

‘She helps fund this little empire does she not?’

‘Aye, that’s the rub. She now wants mair and mair tae dae wie the business and it’s grating on Bob. She wanted tae go wie him tae the Fishermens Union this morning.’

‘Oh, that’s all I need. All we can hope for now is that Willie Dewar doesn’t decide to go higher up.’ Sandra’s mobile ringing prevented her from saying more.

‘Sandra, I’d like a word with you. I’ll be in Fettes tomorrow morning. Oh, and Sandra, bring your warrant card.’

She switched off the phone and looked as if she were about to cry.

CHAPTER FIVE

Tuesday 16th June

She was at her desk in the MIT room when her intercom beeped loudly and a female voice told her to make her way to the Chief's office.

She knocked quietly.

'Sandra, come away in and take a pew.'

'Sir, before…'

'Did you bring your warrant card?'

She opened her satchel and produced the card then leaned across the desk to hand it over.

'The Deputy Chief Inspector turned it this way and that in his finely manicured hand. 'Everything seems to be in order.'

'I don't understand Sir.'

'After the last palaver caused by you losing this,' he held it out, 'I thought it prudent to check to make sure you had it on your person at all times.'

'You know who caused that?'

'Yes, and I would have him remain nameless if it were not for recent developments. What's he up to these days?'

'Still running the investigation agency. What's the big bugger done now, if you don't mind my asking Sir?'

'Nothing too drastic. But then we can but hope. He's only gone and landed himself another consultancy with Police Scotland.'

'What?'

‘I’m afraid so. He starts with you this morning and should be in your office before lunch.’ The Chief leaned over and handed back her warrant card. He has friends in high places that one.’

As Sandra walked towards the door she turned. ‘What about Willie Dewar and the Fishermens Union?’

‘Let’s just say for the sake of clarity that Bob started yesterday.’

She walked back to her office smiling to herself and pondering on the rumour that the Sons of the Widow handshake was all but defunct.

#

Bob was finishing the last drop of his coffee while Rebecca filled the dishwasher. The pair had struggled for conversation throughout breakfast until Bob decided to give it one more go. ‘You’re going to be needed more than ever in the office now Beccy.’

‘And why might that be?’

‘As I told you last night, if you were listening, they’ve offered me a consultancy again, only this time with the murder squad. I’ll remain at the helm of JP course but Tracey will be spending more and more time on her own. Harry is now working full-time with Mrs Spale and Mark is working for Callum and Tod is incarcerated.’

‘You’ll remain at the helm? What about the conflict of interest between JP Associates and your consultancy that you are always banging on about?’

‘That’s exactly why I can’t be seen around the office, but I’ll be there in spirit, if not in person. You’re going to be needed more than ever now. Anyway, must go, I’ve to be in Fettes by eleven.’

Rebecca stood at the window and watched his car draw out before lifting the phone. ‘Tracey, is it okay to join you this morning? You could bring me up to speed on the Molesworth case.’

‘Certainly, Rebecca What time can A expect you?’

‘Shall we say around eleven-thirty? I thought we might manage a bite of lunch down on the Waterfront, on expenses of course.’

‘You are speaking ma language.’

Not quite, thought Rebecca before affirming their meeting.

#

As Bob walked up the stairs into Fettes Command Centre the large aluminium doors opened and out stepped the newly promoted DS Margaret Whalen with the new boss of the Cold Case Squad, DI Sammy Brogue. He and Bob had met once before, when Bob was picking up his personal things from the CCS office.

‘Would you look at what the cat’s dragged in Inspector Brogue. What can we do for you this fine morning Bobby?’

Margaret’s use of the sweetened form of Bob’s name, only ever used by Rebecca, grated on him. ‘It was a fine morning till a moment ago.’

‘No need to be like that, Bobby, after all you’re retired now and have time to enjoy the finer things in life; walks in Cramond and such like.’

‘That’s what I was thinking Margaret, until I received a call yesterday from the high-heid yins to ask me if I could bring my knowledge and expertise to Fettes on a consultancy basis. Of course, I jumped at the chance to work with the murder squad, especially with your friend and mine DI Laing. I started yesterday.’

Inspector Brogue smiled. DS Whalen stumbled and nearly fell down the stairs.

‘Oh and Sandra was just saying last evening at my place before retiring to bed that I was to make sure to pass on her kind regards. She hopes the Cauld Case Squad is managing without her. No insult intended Inspector Brogue.’

'None taken Bob, and good to see you again, it's been a wee while.'

'Aye. Anyway, I'm sure Margaret will have got you up to speed on the CCS, she's always been hot on someone's trail, even if they're deid.' He turned and took the remaining stairs two at a time.

#

'Guess who I met as I was coming into the building?'

'Another Son of the Widow.'

'Now now Sandra.' He sat down on a swivel chair and wheeled it over to Sandra's desk. 'Your friend and mine, Margaret Whalen.'

'You didn't speak to her did you?'

'Not on your life.'

She threw him that familiar look that said aye right. 'By the way, did you know that I was not going to lose my job when I came here this morning? No, don't even bother to answer that, we've enough to be getting on with this morning. Forensics have been down at Molesworth's throughout the night.'

'Did they find anything in the garden?'

#

Rebecca arrived promptly at eleven-thirty. Always one to use power dressing as a means to gain respect, she wore her Barbour jacket over a white blouse, collar up, showing a string of natural pearls. Her grey-green, checked trousers matched the jacket perfectly. Her pink Heathfield Trilby hat, by Barbour, stood out against the rest, and definitely made a statement, especially in Leith.

Tracey made the next statement. 'A see you've been tae the House of Bruar tae.'

Rebecca was completely taken aback by Tracey's knowledge of Bruar fashion that she couldn't speak for some seconds, allowing

Tracey another go. 'Harry took me there in the May weekend and bought me a rig-out.'

'Eventually she caught her breath. 'A what?'

'Claithes. A got a Tweed suit and brogues tae match ma hat.' She pointed to the deerstalker on the coat stand.

Rebecca followed her finger and saw the hat. 'You don't wear that, do you?'

'Well you're wearing that.' Tracey's finger pointed at the pink trilby.

Rebecca's attention was suddenly drawn to Bertie in his basket below the coat stand. 'So this is Bertie. I've heard so much about him.' She stepped forward causing Bertie to rise and growl quietly.

'Has he been trained?'

'Aye. I think it must be your hat.'

She immediately removed her hat and held it behind her back.

'Anywie, make yourself at hame. Where are ye taking me for lunch?'

'I thought maybe Tom Kitchin's. Do you know it?'

'Aye, Harry and I were there for our anniversary. It was magic.'

Rebecca attempted to hide her surprise. 'Oh, really.' She sat down at the coffee table. 'Have we time for a coffee before we go, I've brought us a cheese scone each. I'd like to discuss the Molesworth case.'

'Oh aye, Bob's just off the phone, there's been a right turn-up there.' answered Tracey, 'A'll put the kettle on.' She disappeared into the kitchen.

Bertie continued looking at Rebecca.

'Will Bertie be alright in here with me?' she shouted.

As Tracey was filling the kettle she smiled to herself. 'Aye, he wouldnae hurt a fly.'

#

‘Four bodies, four young women, found under the slabs in the back courtyard, only just buried and no more. It’s a wonder nobody smelled the corpses as they decomposed.’

‘How long have they been there,’ asked Bob.

‘We don’t know yet. George said he thought no more than a year, but we’ll have to await the autopsy results.’

Bob shook his head in disbelief. ‘I thought Molesworth was a cut-throat lawyer, but not to that degree.’

‘We don’t know what he was really like or even if he was the perp.’

‘Oh aye, someone just entered his bedroom, put human ashes in a jug on his dressing-table then dug up the garden and buried four bodies, and all without him knowing. I don’t think so.’

‘Stranger things have happened. Remember Jane Keen? Who’d ever have thought that a well-healed, well-respected Doctor of Psychology, University Lecturer and well-known Counsellor could do what she did?’

‘Very true. That was JP’s first case.’

‘Mm, and my first nightmare. Conflict of interest didn’t come into it.’

‘Aye, so you said often enough at the time. So, what next for the Molesworth case?’

‘I hope you don’t mind my saying Bob James, but have you not just been gainfully employed as my consultant? Maybe a wee bit respect for me wouldn’t go amiss.’

‘Sorry. I’m still not convinced about the Fishermens Union. It’s involved in this in some way.’

‘Why don’t we pay them a visit?’

‘Good idea. Would you mind if we paid the canteen a visit first though; I’ve not seen auld Betty in a while.’

Tracey and Rebecca stood at the reception lectern in Tom Kitchin’s, waiting for a table to become vacant.

‘It is so lovely here,’ said Rebecca, looking around with familiarity.

Before Tracey could reply Tom Kitchin walked up to them. ‘Tracey, nice to see you again. How’s Harry?’

‘Oh Harry, well let’s just say we might not be here for another anniversary.’

‘Like that eh. Let me show you ladies to your table. I’ll prepare a special entre for you both while you decide on the menu.’

As he walked away Tracey called after him. Oh Tom, sorry this is Rebecca.’

Rebecca waited till he’d walked off. ‘How do you know Tom so well?’

‘He came to ma granddaughter’s school tae teach the bairns about cooking.’

‘Did he really?’

‘Aye and we were invited tae. He’s a really nice bloke.’

Rebecca said no more and followed the maître d to their table. ‘Might I suggest the taster menu ladies.’

‘That will dae nicely Charles,’ replied Tracey.

Over the meal the two women discussed JP Associates and Rebecca’s future role before turning their focus on the present case. Tracey explained everything that had happened since the night her and Bob had gone to Molesworth’s and how she thought Sandra Laing may have lost her job that morning.

Rebecca soon put her right on that score. ‘No, Sandra has not lost her job. In fact, she has a new consultant at Fettes.’ She leaned back hoping that one-upmanship counted for women too.

‘How dae you ken that?’

‘Bob received a call last night; did he not tell you? They’ve offered him a consultancy with the murder squad. He accepted.’

‘No, he didnae tell me, but then he disnae live wie me.’

Rebecca ignored the last comment. Oh well, I'd better bring you up to speed.'

#

Sandra and Bob entered the offices of the Fishermens Union just after one o'clock. The receptionist that Bob had met on his last visit was obviously out to lunch and the place seemed deserted. They were about to turn tail and leave when the vestibule door opened behind them and in walked Willie Dewar. He was carrying a Gregg's bag.

'A man after my own heart Willie', said Bob, eyeing the bag.

'You've just eaten two rolls in the police canteen,' said Sandra.

'Good afternoon Bob. Is this another member of JP Associates; I haven't seen her in Greggs. What can I do for you this time?'

'Well you can forget about phoning the police this time for starters. This is Detective Inspector Sandra Laing of the murder squad.'

Sandra did not put her hand forward in greeting. 'Murder Squad, Mr Dewar, because dead bodies are turning up all over the place a mere stone's throw from here. That's not including the body of Charles Molesworth of course.

'If you're here looking for an undertakers there's three in Junction Street.'

'Very funny.'

'I knew Molesworth was a nasty bugger but didn't put him down as a murderer.' Willie squeezed past them to his office. 'I'm going to make a brew, would you like one?'

'Aye that would be very…'

Bob was cut short by Sandra. 'We're not convinced he's a murderer that's why we are here. She turned to face Bob as Willie left the room. 'Remember, let me do the talking.'

'You've done all the talking so far,' answered Bob.

Willie came back grasping a very large mug of tea. The motif on the mug showed a old sailing ship.

'Is that the Marie Celeste,' asked Bob, causing Sandra to shuffle her feet hard on the linoleum.

'Willie turned the mug to look at the image. 'It is that Bob. Are you interested in ships?'

'Not really, though I was born within sight of Granton Harbour. I saw that same image engraved on the glass of your front door.

'A Granton man, well I never.'

'Born and bred.'

'Gentlemen excuse me for interrupting but if you wouldn't mind dispelling with your family history could we get on with the interview.' Sandra sat down at the mahogany desk.

'Am I being interviewed?' asked Willie, turning back to Bob and ignoring Sandra. My family had an office on Lower Granton Road, near the West Pier. Of course we weren't a union then. My family owned fishing trawlers and the engraving on our door then was one of our trawlers. That was before the Government stepped in with its fishing policies. After that our boats, along with all the others on the pier, went for scrap. We removed the glass panel from the door then and had another fitted, engraved with the Marie Celeste. It wasn't long after that we decided to create a union for fishermen, or ex-fishermen to use the correct terminology.'

'I remember your office. My Dad worked for you on the Shore Squad at weekends, landing the fish. I was sent to your office once a week to collect his pay. I must have been about twelve then. There was a wee wall in front of your office that had iron chains linked with metal spikes. In fact, your reception here is very like the one back then too, even down to the wee glass sliding panel on reception.

'We brought that reception with us, along with the front door and had them installed here. Come to think of it I think I remember your Dad. Tam James wasn't it? You're not half like him son.'

'You know if you were there now Willie, you'd be inhabiting the lands of Granton sur Mer and the new Waterfront.'

'Aye, so they tell me. There's no water there by the West Pier now.'

'Right, enough! One more word out of you Bob James and you'll be wishing you had gone to sea. Mr Dewar, how well did you know Charles Molesworth?'

'Apart from the court case and correspondence regarding paying his account, I didn't know him at all.'

'The injured man, what was his name?'

'Brian. Brian Bain.'

'Do you know how he got in contact with Molesworth after his accident?'

'Injured people didn't have to get in touch with Molesworth. He sniffed them out. Apparently, he read all the morning papers and was known to visit the police station and local hospitals. Ambulance chaser extraordinaire.'

'Where is Brian Bain now?'

'He lived in Granton at the time of the accident, but as far as I'm aware he's in a very expensive care home now.'

'As far as you are aware?'

'Well no, I know he is. We foot the bill remember.'

'And where might that home be?'

'Cornucopia. It's in Ravelston Dykes.'

It was Bob's turn. 'Did you know that Mr Molesworth was into Black Magic?'

'How would I know that? It doesn't surprise me mind; nothing about that man would surprise me. He had the mark of the Devil on him that one.'

Sandra threw Bob another of her looks that said the information he'd just given Willie was not for public consumption. 'Is there nothing concrete you can tell us about the deceased that might help us in our enquiries Mr Dewar? Supposition won't get us anywhere.'

He thought for some time. 'Only that the man was never seen around Leith. Never visited the pubs or restaurants and I've heard it said he was somewhat of a recluse, other than his foraging trips to find new clients.'

'Do you know if any of your members knew him?'

'Not that I know of.'

Sandra stood. 'I think we've heard about enough. If you do think of something that might help us, give me a call.' She put a business card on the desk. 'Now if you're ready Mr James?'

'Of course. One question Willie, if your family owned fishing boats you'd have already made your money by the time of the collapse of the Granton fishing industry. Why did you not just take that money and run?'

'They always said I was the black sheep of the family,' answered Willie.

#

As they stepped onto the pavement Sandra looked north towards the docks. She about to wax lyrical about Willie Dewar when an apparition came into view. She could hardly believe her eyes. Walking towards them was Tracey and Rebecca arm in arm. Tracey was wearing a pink trilby and Rebecca sporting a deerstalker. They were both laughing. 'Would you look at this pair coming from the docks.'

Bob was studying the glass panel on the door of the Fishermens Union. He turned and stepped from the entrance way and looked in the direction Sandra was pointing. Old habits die hard and he half expected to see two ladies of the night walk towards him. That's when he did the double-take.

'Hello Bobby, what brings you to this neck of the woods. Or should I say shore?'

'Rebecca, what are you doing here?'

'I work in Leith. Did you forget?'

'So dae I.' said Tracey. 'We thought you'd be spending aw your time at Fettes now, didn't we Rebecca.'

'God forbid,' whispered Sandra.

Bob half expected Tracey to chastise his boss for taking the Lord's name in vain. 'There's working, then there's shirking.?'

'We were researching the locale. After showing Beccy the docks we stopped off for lunch at Kitchin's. Beccy had a Pinot Grigio and A had spring water. We went for the taster menu – magic.'

'We had bacon rolls at Fettes,' added Sandra.

Bob surrendered. 'We've been to see Willie Dewar again. He couldn't tell us much but we now know what happened to Brian Bain, the man who fell in the docks. He was seriously injured after falling between two boats and is in a care home in Ravelston. Coupled with his injuries he has alcoholic dementia so I don't hold out much hope of getting information from him.'

'Aye ye need tae watch out for that when ye get older, especially wie whisky,' said Tracey.

'I know what you mean Tracey,' added Sandra, 'I've seen many an ex-copper go down that road.'

'Alright, alright, can we just dispense with the comedy girls. Where are you two off to now?'

'To our office, where else?' answered Rebecca.

Sandra smiled broadly. 'We're going to the care home to see if we can see this Bain character.' She touched Bob on the shoulder. 'Come on Big Man,' then crossed the road towards the Links.

‘We’ll have a look at those shallow graves at Molesworth’s before we head to Ravelston.’

#

Callum Mackie and his only employee, Doctor of Psychology, Mark le Mot were only hours away from meeting their first clients. BEYOND, their drug rehabilitation programme at the Grassick Centre off Coburg Street – a mere stone’s throw from the banks of the Water of Leith was now open for business.

The centre was named after Callum’s old military comrade, friend and lobster fisherman Sandy Grassick whose legacy gave Callum a large house in Trinity and the finance to open the centre.

As he looked from the top floor window onto the river Callum spoke, as if to no-one in particular. ‘I sometimes wonder if those poor people addicted to drugs have much chance in life. What can we really do to keep them from that river? There is no magic fix.’

‘It’s beginning to sound as if you don’t have much belief in BEYOND Callum.’ Mark was thumbing through the books on their newly acquired bookshelves. ‘I had to read each of these tomes, and get to know each writer before I was even accepted to do my PhD.’

‘And here am I, a mere man of God with only a theology degree to my name.’ Callum turned from the window.

‘You could try praying?’

‘Is this secular sarcasm I hear? I heard a lot about praying when I was a practising minister and saw it working too. Let’s just hope that between the two of us we can help the poor sods who find their way here. I’ve had a meeting with BETHANY and it has agreed to put our leaflets up in their hostels and hand them out at the Care Van.’

‘Tracey volunteers on the care van on Friday evenings.’

‘Aye, she’s a great woman Tracey. I met with her recently. JP Associates is wrapped up in another case. This one involves the occult in some way. Tracey was asking my opinion.’

‘What is your opinion?’

‘It would be amiss of me to refute the idea of spirits when I worship one. Wouldn’t it Dr le Mot.’

Mark smiled. He should have known that Callum could never be caught out with such a misleading question.

‘What are your thoughts on the subject Mark?’

‘Not much really but the university has a department dedicated to the paranormal and some of my fellow students got involved.

‘What, ghost-hunting and the like?’

‘I think so. They may have touched on spiritual readings and seances too. Did you know that Arthur Conan Doyle was a follower of esoteric beliefs? There is a centre dedicated to his work on the subject in Palmerston Place. Sophie mentioned something to me about a Mr Molesworth being haunted. What was he up to?’

‘Not much to tell really, except that he was found dead and in a terrible condition. It looked as if he’d been frightened to death. His Rottweiler dog was still alive but Tracey had never seen a dog in such a state. It was as if it had seen something beyond normal. It was shaking uncontrollably and would not move from its basket.’

‘Goodness me…’

The sound of BEYOND’s doorbell ringing stopped Mark in his tracks. Callum headed for the lift. ‘That might be our first client. If it is I’ll show them up. As Callum disappeared, Mark took his lounge chair by the small, round coffee table. He was hardly in his chair when the realisation of what he was about to do dawned on him. His neck tightened slightly and he felt somewhat agitated.’

He waited like this for more than ten minutes, believing that Callum must be busy putting the client at ease, when his mobile rang. *'Mark, I've nipped out for a little while. Oh, and Mark, you can relax, it's Valerie.'*

The young psychologist smiled at his boss's ability to read minds then walked over to the bookshelves and chose a book. BEYOND GOOD & EVIL. He moved to the window and looked down. On the path directly below stood Callum and Valerie. She looked as if she'd been crying.

#

Rebecca and Tracey were still laughing as they got to the office. Tracey took the key from her handbag to unlock the door. At this point Bertie the bloodhound should have been jumping against the door in excitement, but he wasn't. The key wouldn't budge in the lock either. She put her hand above her eyes to see past her own reflection in the glass. 'Bertie's not there. Maybe Bob's taken, no he couldn't have, he's with Sandra.'

She thought hard on who else might have a key to the office. Then she remembered there was another key holder, and she was standing beside her. 'Have you got your key on ye?'

'Yes.'

'Give it a try in the lock before A phone Bob.'

The lock didn't budge.

'Bob, we cannae get into the office, and Bertie's gone.'

'How do you know if you can't get into the office?'

'Don't be smart. He's not come tae the door.'

'Tracey, I'm up to my eyes in it. What's going on.'

'The lock is jammed and there is no sign of Bertie.'

There was a long silence before Bob replied. *'I'll be there asap.'*

'What did he say?' asked Rebecca.

'He sounds harassed, but he'll be here shortly.'

‘Harassed or not, he’s taken a real liking to Bertie.’

‘Aye, he’s coming tae rescue Bertie, never mind about us.’

Tracey knew what asap meant but didn’t expect an unmarked police car, siren blaring, to screech across Great Junction Street and stop at the bus stop facing the oncoming traffic. Sandra and Bob got quickly out of the car. ‘Still no sign of Bertie?’

Rebecca smiled at Tracey. ‘He does love that dog.’

‘No, and we still can’t budge the lock.’

Bob put his nose to the keyhole. ‘Superglue; some bastard has put superglue in the lock!’

‘That still doesn’t explain Bertie being missing.’ As Tracey said this she heard a dog bark. It came from the direction of the Kirkgate. ‘That’s him. A’d ken that bark anywhere.’

Sandra was immediately off at speed before any of the others had moved.

‘She used to race for the Edinburgh Harriers,’ said Bob.

As they followed her towards the Kirkgate Sandra walked towards them. In her left hand she held Bertie’s lead and in her right the collar of a teenager. ‘Here’s the culprit. And it looks as if Bertie was not the only thing that took his interest in your office.’

The boy was holding a black plastic bag.

Bob took the bag and opened it to find the office diary and a pile of receipts. ‘What did you want with these son? You wouldn’t get anything for them.’

‘It wisnae me.’

‘Oh I see. How could we have made such a mistake? Oh aye, the dog, the diary and our paperwork. Did you find them in the bin there by the bus-stop?’

‘A man asked me tae dae it. He gave me fifty quid.’

‘Fifty pounds,’ said Sandra. ‘That’s a lot of money. Did it include jamming the lock so these ladies couldn’t get in their office?’

‘Aye. He told me what tae dae, then A was tae meet him in the Links; that’s where A was gaun when ye caught me.’

Sandra gripped his collar harder and turned him around. ‘Right son, let’s go and see if we can find the gentleman in question. And if you’re lying to us, it will be the high jump for you.’ She handed Bertie’s lead to Tracey and began marching the boy towards the Links.

Bob followed, then turned around. ‘Get in touch with a locksmiths and see if they can get into the office.’

‘Yes Sir, answered Rebecca.’

Bob shook his head and moved quickly away.

‘I’m not sure he liked that,’ said Tracey, bending down to stroke Bertie. Good boy, you’ve caught your first criminal.

‘No, probably not,’ answered Rebecca.

#

Mark turned from the window and sat down hard in the lounge chair. The book remained closed on his knee as he pondered on the last few months since gaining his PhD. From his perspective he’d gained nothing since and had even begun contemplating whether Callum’s offer of employment was mere charity, or a way of clearing his conscience. He’d not been the same since the death of Sandy Grassick and since then seemed hell-bent on doing good works, or in colloquial parlance, being a do-gooder, almost to the point where it could be said that he was covering something up.

Certainly, Valerie’s painting of the fisherman and his boat and the strange white substance she’d painted inside the man’s lobster creels, coupled with the very large drugs haul discovered at Newhaven Harbour just after Sandy’s death had everyone in JP’s talking, all except Callum, who'd completely buttoned-up on the subject.

Mark stood, put the book back on the shelf and made himself a coffee, before going back to the window.

'I just don't know what to think, or do Callum.'

'It's a lot to take in Val. Have you been to see him?'

'He doesn't want me to visit, he's so ashamed of what he did.'

Callum continued looking at the murky river. 'It was all in the name of good government as far as I know.'

'Do you believe he really was working for MI5?'

'I did hear that.'

'Then how could he have ended up in jail for murder?'

'Quite easily. The powers that be occasionally require operatives as scapegoats, it helps take the focus off its own acts. On this occasion that operative is Tod Peterson.'

'I don't believe this Government would do that.'

'But then you work for it, don't you? One only has to look to the soldiers who've been put on trial for actions committed in war situations that were not instigated by them.'

'Are you talking about yourself Callum?'

He turned to face her. 'They didn't get as far as arresting me, but they did come close after the Falklands; many Argentinian soldiers lost their lives, some say unnecessarily. Interestingly enough, no political leaders went to jail for the sinking of the Belgrano. It was the same after the Bosnian conflict, everyone was looking for scapegoats.'

'I read about that. Wasn't that lawyer who was found dead recently involved in the Bosnian War trials in the Hague?'

'How do you know that?'

'When I was an art student I was working with patients at the Andrew Duncan Clinic and he was one of them.'

'What a small world we live in Valerie. So you met him?'

'We spoke a time or two. He had some very interesting things to say about what had gone on during the conflict. Apparently, he learned it all from a young witness who subsequently got killed in a hit and run before the actual trial.'

Callum looked at his watch. Jings, is that the time? Look Valerie, I'll have to go but if you wish I can visit Tod the next time I'm at Saughton and talk some sense into him.'

'Would you do that for me?'

'On one condition; you agree to have dinner with me tonight at the Starbank, just for old times' sake.'

'Oh Callum, I'm not…'

'Mark will be there of course.'

She put her arm through his. 'Better make it the Shore Bar then, he just adores their olive platter.'

#

It only took Bob, Sandra and their reluctant prisoner ten minutes to reach Leith Links.

The teenager pointed across the park. 'He said tae meet him over there at the dressing rooms.'

'What does he look like?' asked Bob.

'He was tall and skinny and had on a black suit and black polo neck. He was really scary and telt me if A didnae dae what A was told he would find me and naebody would ever see me again.'

'And you believed him?' asked Sandra.

'You'd have believed him tae. A'm no daft, he really meant it.'

As they made their way across the grass, Bob saw the black van he'd seen the previous day with Tracey. It was parked adjacent to the dressing rooms. He watched as it pulled away. 'Hold it Sandra. No point in going any further.'

'What do you mean?'

'You see that van,' he pointed at the disappearing vehicle. 'I'm sure the man in question is driving it.'

‘How could you possibly know that; the windows are blacked out.’

‘I’ve seen it, and the driver before.’

‘Where?’

‘Here. I think JP Associates is being stalked. Either that or he’s a member of a dog thieving gang. The last time Tracey and I saw him it looked as if he was after Bertie.’ Bob turned to the youngster. ‘How did you get into the office?’

He put his hand into his tracksuit pocket and produced a set of keys. Bob recognised the VW fob immediately.

‘Let him go Sandra, he’s no use to us now, but we’d better get to Tod’s place asap.’

They were there in no time and expected to see a broken door, or at least, a wide-open door but although the vestibule doors were open, Tod’s flat door was tightly closed. Sandra looked through the letterbox.

‘No need to do that Sandra, we’ve got the keys, remember.’

‘Oh aye, of course.’

‘Not the onset of alcoholic dementia I hope?’

‘Very funny!’

Once in the flat they looked around for signs of a break-in but everything was in its place including the dust. Sandra picked up the newspaper lying on the settee. ‘A Guardian reader I see.’

‘That’s Tod, always one for the people.’

‘Do you think that’s why he murdered Richard Stark? Maybe he couldn’t take the greed? Do you know that in the bible greed is represented many times as idolatry?’

‘The Guardian is only a newspaper Sandra. You can’t go building a case on its readership. Anyway, where did you get the biblical references, you’ve not been in a church for a long time, as far as I know?’

‘I was in one last Sunday and the sermon was about greed.’

‘Well I never. What were you doing there?’

‘That’s personal.’

‘Aye, alright. On the subject of Tod then, do you not believe Peter Blue when he says he was working for the Security Services?’

‘Quite honestly, no.’

‘Do you believe that Richard Stark was a threat to the nation?’

‘That’s a hard pill to swallow too. He was merely a banker for God’s sake.’

‘A banker who could have brought down the Government if he’d been allowed to continue.’

Sandra merely shook her head. ‘Anyway, how did Tod’s keys end up in the hands of that teenager?’

‘Check the dust on the shelf just inside the front door. That’s where Tod’s keys sat. Someone’s put a straightened coat hanger through the letter box and hooked the keys. There’s been a spate of thefts like that recently. It’s a wonder Tod’s car is still outside, they’ve got his car key too. Wait a minute, my house key is on Tod’s bunch.’

‘Looks like we got that young thief in the nick of time eh.’

‘Sandra, who the fuck is stalking us?’

‘I’ve no idea, but whoever it is, I wouldn’t like to get on the wrong side of them, they’re not daft, that’s for sure. If they’ve had time to copy your key, you might have to stay in Portobello with me until we catch whoever it is.’

‘I wondered when you’d get round to that.’

‘Aye, so you did. In your dreams Big Boy.’

CHAPTER SIX

Wednesday 17th June

Bob was up at his usual 6am and making the first brew of the day when Sandra, still in dressing gown, came into the kitchen. 'So, what did Rebecca really say about you coming back here?'

'I've told you already. Rebecca is fine with it. Sophie was more upset than her mother.'

'You better be telling the truth. Is that a pot of coffee you're making?'

As Sandra said this, there was a loud knock on the front door.

'I'll get it,' said Bob, moving quickly from the kitchen.

When he opened the door there was no-one there. He walked to the gate, leaned over and looked both ways; still nothing. As he turned to walk back into the house he saw that Sandra had followed him out, dressing gown and all. She was holding a postcard up for him to see. 'I thought postcards were a thing of the past,' she said.

Bob squinted. 'What is it?'

'It's a painting of a handgun.'

'A what?' Then it dawned on him. He rushed past her and made for the bedroom. Opening the chest of drawers he removed some towels. The handgun was there, where he'd left it. Sandra looked around him and saw the gun.

'Is that a handgun you've got in there?'

'Sandra, I can explain.'

‘I’m sure you can, but can you explain this?’ She held up the postcard again. Written on the opposite side from the picture were the words “BANG BANG”. She turned to the picture. ‘That’s an exact replica of yours’

‘The bastard has been in the house already.’

‘Mm, now what are we going to do about you having an illegal firearm in your possession? If they’d taken this firearm you’d be in deep shit.’

#

‘I didn’t expect my pastoral care to arrive in such a familiar guise,’ said Tod.

‘Kirk Ministers are like paratroopers; we land when one least expects it.’

‘It’s good to see you Callum.’

‘Good to see you too Tod. How are they treating you?’

‘Not bad at all considering. I miss my old friend though.’

‘Bob?’

‘No, old John Barleycorn.

Callum put his hand into the inside pocket of his jacket, removed a half bottle of whisky and looked around before passing it over. ‘They never think to search Ministers. Though I must say, it doesn’t look as if abstinence is doing you much harm. You’re looking well.’

‘Maybe. Did you know I teach literacy classes on Wednesday evenings?’

‘I did not.’

‘Tracey assists me. It’s a much-needed skill in here particularly when people are released.’

‘Does Jimmy take part?’

‘He does. He’s handy to have around is Jimmy. The other eleven learners wouldn’t dare wind me up when he’s there.’ He leaned back in his chair.

‘I’ve come to speak to you about Valerie.’

‘I thought that might be the case. No such thing as a free dram. What about her?’

‘She’s missing you.’

‘How do you know?’

‘She told me. She would like to visit but thinks you’re against it. She came to see me yesterday. The lass can’t understand why you don’t want to see her and neither can I for that matter.’

‘You can’t?’

‘Well, maybe I can but you have a motive for what you did. That might be worth explaining to her.’

‘What I did was wrong.’

‘Not if it was in the name of Her Majesty.’

‘Oh, not you as well.’

‘What?’

‘Me, an MI5 operative? Bob has been banging on about that for months too.’

‘A perfect alibi, don’t you think.’

‘But not true.’

‘So, you say, but it is according to Peter Blue, and he should know being ex-head of the service.’

‘I don’t get this. Why would he lie to save me?’

‘To be honest I think it’s more to do with Daniel Manning. He’s taken a shine to you and probably put in a word.’

Tod thought for a moment. ‘You used to work for Peter, didn’t you?’

‘That was a long time ago.’

‘Was it he who told you I’d worked for him?’

‘No, it was Tracey.’

‘Tell me the truth Callum, do you believe any of this sorry tale?’

‘It’s neither here nor there what I believe. Remember that night you came to see me? You all but put your cards on the table then.

What is important now is that you have a future with Valerie and it's what she believes that counts. She's a good woman Tod, and perfectly suited to a man whose name conjures up images of old Nick.'

'I can't believe I'm hearing this from a clergyman. Did you know Valerie calls me Dougal Douglas, a character of Muriel Spark's? Sometimes I think she does believe I'm part devil.'

'I remember I told you that when we first met. She told me the same last night in the Shore Bar.'

'You were in the Shore Bar?'

'Now, don't go getting jealous. I took her and Mark for their tea.'

For the first time since Callum's arrival Tod looked decidedly sad.

'I'm sorry Tod, I didn't mean to…'

'No, don't worry about it. And thanks for coming.' Tod stood.

'Are you going to let her come to see you?'

Tod walked away without replying.

#

If Callum had not been looking down at his feet as he walked from the prison he might have seen Bob James go in. If he'd stayed around, even a short while, he might have seen him leave again for his wasn't a social visit. He was there for only one purpose, he wanted a piece of information and it only took him five minutes to tell Tod about the stalker and ask how they could enlist the help of Daniel Manning.

Earlier that day he'd had to explain to Sandra how the firearm came into his possession, though he did not divulge the source. That would never do, he thought as his mind turned to DI Jackie Gould. That didn't stop her emphasising more than once that he had only escaped a charge by surrendering that firearm to her. What she was going to do with it she wouldn't say.

#

Tracey did manage to get a local locksmith to attend to their wee problem that afternoon, whilst she and Rebecca retired to Wetherspoons for coffee.

CHAPTER SEVEN

Thursday 18th June

Bob took the slope that led down into Waverley Station at pace but even before he reached the concourse he could see the vagrant leaning with his back to the metal parapet.

'Are you here to move me on Inspector?'

'If I was still an Inspector you'd be nicked and it would be for more than vagrancy.'

'No need to be like that. So, what do I owe the pleasure at this early hour.'

'I, we need your help.'

'Mm. And the "we" are?'

'JP Associates.'

'Oh, of course you're a man down. Am I being offered a job?'

'Not quite. We need your expertise to help us track someone.'

'What have they done?'

Bob sat down beside him. 'They're stalking us, with what I believe to be evil intent.'

'Now that does sound right up my street, evil intent. Have you mentioned this to Peter?'

'No.'

'Why not?'

'I think you know why not. He'll go off on one about his beloved niece Rebecca being in danger and start using all sorts of threats to close us down.'

'Yep, that sounds like Uncle Peter. By the way, how did you find me? No, don't answer that. There's only one person knows my pitch. So, you've been to see him?'

'He's bearing up.'

'Good. And how's Valerie?'

'I'm not sure. She hasn't been to see Tod.'

'Does she want too?'

'I'm not sure about that either.'

'He's a good man Tod. Every time he visited me here he always got me a coffee.'

'Aye, that's Tod for you,' said Bob, standing up. 'Oh, one other thing Daniel, we don't want anything too drastic to happen to the stalkers, we merely want to find out who they are. Enjoy your day.'

#

Sandra and Bob had arranged to meet mid-morning at Fettes. The gun had not been mentioned again, other than her telling him she'd handed it in to the firearms unit as a lost and found item.

As they passed reception Bob took hold of Sandra's arm. 'What about the canteen first? I'm starving.'

'You've had your breakfast already.'

'What call that breakfast, a bowl of Muesli and a cup of English breakfast tea?'

'Right, but we've only got twenty minutes.'

As they entered the canteen Sandra walked up to the counter. She looked back. 'Full Scottish?'

'No, just get me a blackpudding and egg doubler and another on slice sausage; brown sauce on both.'

'It's a wonder you're not twenty stone with the food you put away?'

'This body's a temple,' answered Bob, before spotting Margaret Whalen sitting with a young female constable. He recognised the WPC as the one who'd attempted to arrest him for drink driving. It was Sandra's niece. 'I see Margaret has taken a shine to your niece.'

Sandra turned and looked over to their table in time to see Bob walk towards it.

'Mind if I join you girls?' He didn't wait for an answer but pulled out a chair and sat down. 'Hello Daphne, it's been a while. Your Auntie's just getting them in. Would either of you like a refill?'

Margaret was first to answer. 'No thank you.'

'It would help keep you warm in your office. Did they ever get that heating fixed?' Bob knew that his Nemesis couldn't bear that her ex colleague was now consultant with MIT.

She didn't answer.

'Sandra was just saying over an early morning cuppa this morning how a nice cup of tea can warm the cockles.'

Margaret stood and was about to go when Sandra arrived with Bob's breakfast. She made a show of serving him using all the feminine charm she could muster. He resisted saying thank you darling, but was very tempted.

'Is DS Whalen looking after you alright Daphne? I think you'll find the Cold Case Squad very interesting.'

'I only started with DS Whalen last week Auntie and I'm still finding my feet.'

Her niece's reply told Sandra all she needed to know; her niece was not being nurtured in a way that befitted a WPC new to a particular position. 'Maybe DS Whalen will fill you in on the details of our previous cases, some which involved a private investigation firm, JP Associates. Bob here is one of the proprietors, I believe you met a while back. His partner is indisposed at the minute but I'm sure Bob would be more than happy to take some time to explain how the police and public work together towards a shared goal, namely putting the wrong people away. Bob is an ex-Detective Inspector and now a consultant with MIT.'

Bob could swear that he saw Margaret sink lower in her chair.'

#

As he followed his boss into the MIT main office a loud applause filled the room. Every detective stood to welcome their old colleague. Those who'd never met him but heard of him stood too.

The office was a tad different from the freezing cold basement room set aside for the Cold Case Squad. For one thing in MIT there were twelve desks each with a desktop computer. This contrasted with the one computer between three desks in CCS.

DS John Mackay walked up to Bob and shook his hand. 'Welcome back Sir.' It seemed to Bob that John had not yet taken his lesson from Sandra about never referring to his ex-boss as Sir.

That caused him to smile. 'Good to see you too John. How's the racing going?'

'I've qualified for the Borders Rally. It's this weekend if you're interested?'

'I think I've seen enough of your rallying skills in the Borders, don't you?'

They both laughed out loud at Bob's subtle reference to the Gormand case, a case and a journey that saw them follow Gormand to his subsequent death.

Sandra's loud voice interrupted their camaraderie. 'Now ladies and gents when you've done with the bonding can we get down to the job in hand.' She stopped, removed her coat, threw it across her desk and walked up to the chalkboard. 'Bob and I visited the site of the burials in Molesworth's garden in Queen Charlotte Street yesterday. Has there been any word back from forensics yet?'

Just as she'd asked this the Chief Inspector walked into the room. 'Word arrived only ten minutes ago. Each of the four bodies have been dead for no longer than six months. Four females - all were in the early to mid-twenties. There is no sign of foul play, as yet, and you'll be the first to know when the cause of death is established. How far have we got to date Inspector Laing?'

'I was just about to recap with the team Sir if you'd care to stay around?'

'Not possible I'm afraid. I've another meeting at Waverley Court with the Council. Bloody Edinburgh Partnership!' He turned to go. 'Leave a note on my desk. I'll see it this afternoon.'

Sandra took a moment to gather her thoughts. 'Right where are we.' She turned back to the flip-chart and began writing.

MOLESWORTH'S BODY DISCOVERED IN THE EARLY HOURS OF TUESDAY 9TH JUNE. HE LOOKED AS IF HE'D DIED OF SHOCK.

THE SAME DAY AN OCCULT HEXOGRAM IS DISCOVERED DRAWN ON HIS ATTIC FLOOR.

TUESDAY 16TH JUNE THE BODIES OF FOUR FEMALES DISCOVERED UNDER SLABS IN MOLESWORTH'S GARDEN.

'And as we've just learned, if you'd been listening to our leader, those bodies have been there for approximately six months. As you may or may not know prior to his demise Molesworth had visited JP Associates offices in Great Junction Street early on Monday 8th June to ask for help; he believed he was being haunted. And no, I don't want to hear a peep about ghost busters or conflict of interest or any other such dribble, we are all part of the same team in here.'

'The investigation agency had not had time to bring their skills into play before their client was found dead the following morning, and as I have said he did look as if he'd seen a ghost.'

A young detective raised his hand.

'We are not in school now Thomas so no need for the hand, but I'm not quite finished.' She walked from the chart to stand amongst them. 'Now what I am about to tell you is in the strictest of confidence, and that is for your ears too Kathryn.' Kathryn, the oldest detective in the room, was famed for liking a blether to all and sundry. 'The staff of JP Associates are being stalked by person or persons unknown. As yet we are no further forward in knowing who they are or what their goal is. So far, they have burgled Bob's office and Bob's partner Thomas Peterson's house, where they got the office keys and the keys to Bob's house and have been there too. For want of a better lead, I want this treated as part of the investigation into the Queen Charlotte Street deaths.' She looked at Kathryn. 'And if it should get to the ears of our beloved Chief, you know what will happen to the perpetrator.'

It was Bob's turn to step to the wall chart. 'Thank you Inspector. If I can make one more thing clear. JP Associates will be using police time in their investigation into the death of their client Charles Molesworth. Our agency had no intention of bringing this case to your door, but that was only until murder was mentioned and since it has any assistance would be much appreciated.' He was about to step aside when he heard a loud cough and immediately noticed an old acquaintance among the detectives. 'Well Ross, what happened to you? Special Branch send you packing?'

Subdued laugher rose amongst the gathering.

'Pleased to see you too Bob.'

'How's the handicap these days, the golfing one, not your personality?'

'Right gentlemen,' interrupted Sandra, 'Thomas I believe you have a question for us. What is it you would like to know?'

#

Sandra and Bob left Fettes just after one o'clock and decided to take a walk in Inverleith Park before heading back to Molesworth's. They discussed their visit to Brian Bain in the care-home in Ravelston two days before and how it had produced nothing worth writing down. The man, whoever he'd been, was well gone. buried somewhere behind the nullifying effects of alcoholic dementia.

Sandra repeated that she didn't hold out much hope of her team getting any nearer finding out who was stalking JP Associates and it soon became obvious to him that she was at the end of her tether.

She bent down and picked a small tuft of new summer grass and put it to her nose. 'I think we'd better go back to Molesworth's and have a more in-depth look at the house and grounds.'

Bob watched her closely and was tempted to make a joke but something in her demeanour prevented him. 'Forensics have already done that Sandra.'

'Aye, but we know how the science boys can miss the obvious. It takes detectives to get to the nitty-gritty, unless of course you're a Silent Witness fan. That lot don't seem to need the police at all.'

'I know what you mean but I still don't see the point. Anyway, 'll need to go to the office first to see that Tracey is okay, especially with the stalker somewhere in the vicinity.'

'Why do I always get the impression you don't want to go to Molesworth's house?'

'Don't be daft woman. I'll be with you there ASAP.'

#

As Bob opened the office door he was about to wax lyrical about Sandra then saw the elderly lady seated at the coffee table.

'Bob this is Mrs Molesworth, Charles's Mum. Charles told her he'd be coming to see us.'

He closed the door and walked straight to the coffee table and sat down. 'Mrs Molesworth, I am so pleased to meet you though sorry it is in such dreadful circumstance.'

'Mrs Molesworth was telling me all about her son.'

He could see the old lady had been crying.

'Charles was such a lovely boy and not what the newspapers and television made him out to be at all.'

Tracey threw Bob a look that said, Do not dare contradict her.

'He really cared about the people he represented. Do you know that he spent time at the War Crimes Tribunals in The Hague? He was highly respected back then. It was only after he was forced to retire from that position that he set up business in Leith and it was after that the slurs began.'

'When did he set up in business Mrs Molesworth?' asked Bob.

'You can call me Elizabeth please. I think it was around 1998. He'd only been married about a year.'

'We didn't know he had been married,' said Tracey.

'He still is. He was quite ill when he met Jo. She was a psychiatric nurse in Andrew Duncan Hospital and helped him recover. We thought she was a lovely girl. My husband was alive then and he took a real shine to her.'

'Where is she now?'

Mrs Molesworth ignored the question. 'We're not sure what caused the change but within a few years of marriage it became obvious that she did not want children and had begun going out on her own. Since then they've been living separate lives. She has her own house at Leith Links. Charles couldn't bear the thought of divorce so they agreed to remain married. I must say this has benefitted Jo greatly. She has never worked since the day they parted and Charles footed the bill for her very expensive lifestyle. It was that which in the end caused him to pursue accident cases. The truth was, he needed the money.'

Bob stood. 'This shines a whole new light on your son, Mrs…Elizabeth. Tracey will you get Elizabeth a nice cup of tea and maybe even a wee doughnut. I'm meeting Sandra at Charles's house. Before I go thought Elizabeth, you don't happen to have his wife's address?'

'I wrote it out earlier in case you needed it.' She handed him a slip of paper.

He called to the kitchen. 'Tracey, would you mind if Bertie came with me?'

Bertie jumped from his basket and began wagging his tail.

'He really likes you,' said Mrs Molesworth, as Bob and Bertie left the office. 'He's such a nice man your partner,' she called to Tracey as the front door closed.

She could hear the reply.

#

'You took your time.'

'Sorry Sandra, I was held up.'

'Hope they didn't get away with much. Have you been taking Bertie for a walk?'

'Very funny. I brought him here to see if he picks up any scent or such like. He is a bloodhound after all.'

'At last, a relevant contribution to the case.'

'Let's wait and see.' He led Bertie up the stairs but the second he opened Molesworth's bedroom door the dog began to snarl and refused to enter the room.

Bob pulled on his lead. 'Come on Bertie.'

But Bertie was having none of it and pulled the other way.

Sandra pushed past them into the room. 'I thought I could smell this last time we were here; capsaicin.'

'What are you on about?'

'Do you not remember it from your training days at Tulliallan? It's pepper spray.'

'That's it. I did think I could smell something that night.'

'What night? You weren't here at night. You're getting auld Bob James.'

'Aye, so I am,' stammered Bob, having completely forgotten that no-one, other than Tracey and Rebecca and Sophie knew he'd been there the night of Molesworth's death. He deemed a change of subject very necessary. 'Molesworth has a mother.'

'That's nice.'

'She's in the office with Tracey at the moment.'

'And you weren't going to tell me?'

'He has a wife too.'

'What?'

'I would have thought your lot would have made enquiries regarding his next of kin?'

'You thought right, they should have. Somebody back in Fettes is going to get their balls chewed off.'

'Lucky devil.'

'So, what about this mother? And where's the wife?'

'According to Molesworth's Mum, her son was an angel in disguise, it was his wife Jo that was the money-grabber.'

'Is she still his wife?'

'No, he's dead, she's his widow.'

'Right, cut the comedy!'

Bob reached into the inside pocket of his jacket and produced Mrs Molesworth's note. 'She lives just across the Links from here. This puts a whole new meaning on his death don't you think?'

'What are we waiting for then?'

#

Tracey was putting on her coat ready to leave for the day when there was a loud knock on the front door. She turned quickly but there was no-one there. 'Schoolbairns,' she mumbled as she walked to the desk for her handbag. When she turned round to leave there was a woman standing inside the door.

'Can A help ye?'

'I hope so. My husband told me he'd come to see you, and that was just before he died. I'm Jo Molesworth.'

Bob and Sandra rang Jo Molesworth's doorbell continuously but no one answered. 'She's maybe at work?' said Sandra, lifting the letter box to peer in.

'Not as far as Mrs Molesworth knows. She said that her daughter-in-law had never worked since meeting her son and that she was draining him of everything he had. That's why he ended up chasing ambulances, according to her.'

'On the other hand, that's a mothers-in-law for you. What about children?'

'I still can't believe you're asking me this. Surely you have a file on Molesworth?'

'Of sorts.'

'Right Sandra, would you care to tell me what is really going on here! This is just not like you.'

She looked around before answering. 'Keep your voice down Bob.'

'What is it?'

'I'm not very well.'

'Are you not coping?'

'With the job? Yes. At least I was. No it's me, they think I might have breast cancer.'

Bob was silent for a moment. Who are they?'

'The NHS Consultant. He's doing tests.'

'How long have you known?'

'Since the Tuesday we discovered our Mr Molesworth. I've hardly been able to concentrate since.'

'You could have put John Mackay in charge of the case?'

‘So I could. He’s a good driver Bob, but I’m not so sure about him leading a murder investigation. He’s still a wee bit wet behind the ears.’

‘I could keep an eye on him. You should really take some time off.’

‘And leave you two to your own devices? No, I don’t think so, you’d enjoy the praise too much “Sir”.

‘It would be the only praise I get these days. What’s the prognosis?’

‘If it’s malignant they’re talking about an operation and chemo. That could put me out for months, or longer. My sick pay would run out and where would that leave me?’

Better than dead, Bob didn’t say. ‘Well what about just taking a back seat? We could cover for you.’

‘I’ll have to think about it. Maybe one consultant under my hair is enough for the moment.’

#

‘A was just leaving for the day.’

‘It won’t take long.’

Tracey returned her handbag to the floor behind the desk but kept her coat on. ‘I’m Tracey Cowan, company secretary, amongst other things.’

‘Keeper of secrets.’

‘What?’

‘That’s what it means, “secretary”, the keeper of secrets.’

Tracey began to dislike Jo Molesworth.

Jo put out her hand in greeting.

Her dislike grew and she sat down behind the desk, without shaking the proffered hand. ‘A believe you might keep some secrets yourself Jo?’

‘And what might those be? Oh of course, I saw Charles’s Mum leave here a short while ago.’

‘If you’d care to hang around, I could phone my boss; he’d could be here in a few minutes.’

‘Would that be Mr James? I believe he is at my front door as we speak.’

‘How dae ye know that?’

‘You obviously don’t. I believe it always pays to be vigilant. I have a spy-cam above my front door that is linked to my mobile and it sends me a signal if someone presses my door-bell, letting me see on video who my visitor is, or are in Bob’s case, he has a lady with him.’ She turned the screen to Tracey.

‘That ain’t no lady Jo, that is Detective Inspector Sandra Laing.’

If Jo was worried she didn’t show it. ‘I only popped in after seeing Charles’s Mum leave. I wanted to give you my side of the story after some things you may have been told by his Mum. She has never liked me and still blames me for stealing her beloved son and I’m sure she would have painted a picture of a wonderful son. I suppose one can’t blame her for that.’ Jo looked as if she was about to cry. ‘I am sorry that Charles is dead but if truth be told, he was a terrible man. We met when he was in hospital suffering from mental illness. He’d had a severe breakdown during the war crimes trials in The Hague. His mother believes it was dealing with the aftermath of the atrocities that caused his breakdown, but it wasn’t. I didn’t think it prudent to share the truth with her. His father was not long dead and I felt it was more than she could have coped with.’

Another practitioner of benevolent lying, thought Tracey. ‘What did happen in the Hague?’

‘There was a young woman, a victim of war crimes and a witness to events in Bosnia; she was only seventeen. Charles had to interview her several times, which led to him meeting her outside of office hours and taking her to his hotel. After some months she threatened to tell the authorities, unless he gave her money.'

'Did he give her money?'

'On the day he went to the bank to get the first payment he left her at a table by a roadside café. As he was coming from the bank a truck mounted the pavement and the girl was killed outright. He saw her under the wheel of the truck and he collapsed on the street. When he woke he was in hospital. Of course, no-one put two and two together and he was eventually transferred here where it was decided that psychiatric care would be most relevant course of action. If truth be told he should have been arrested.'

'And that's where you came in?'

'Yes.'

'And Charles told you willingly what had happened.'

'No, not at first, and not to the doctors in hospital. It was after he was released and we had married that he decided to confide in me.'

'And you forgave him.'

'I didn't think there was anything to forgive really, not then; the girl wasn't underage and was obviously on the make. No, the need to forgive came much later, once I discovered that Charles's penchant for young girls didn't just stretch to the Hague. He like the Leith girls too. At first, I decided to turn a blind eye because I loved him and was hoping for a family. But a family was the last thing he wanted.'

'Did ye never challenge him about it.'

'What was the point. Once he recovered from his trauma he made it clear he was his own man. I felt sorry for his Mum, she really did believe in him, but I couldn't take anymore of him and eventually bucked up the courage to leave. We agreed, for the sake of his Mum and his reputation with the legal establishment, that we would not divorce and in return I accepted a settlement.'

Tracey suddenly put her hand forward to shake Jo's. 'I am sorry Jo, that was not the story his Mum told.'

'No, she couldn't, she doesn't know, poor woman.'

'Listen, A hope ye don't mind but A've got tae go. The grandbairn comes for her tea on Thursdays.'

'You have children?'

'Aye, and their children tae.'

Jo looked solemn as she turned to walk to the door. 'Thanks for listening.'

'Nae bother. Oh, one thing Jo, I can call you Jo?'

'Of course.'

'How did ye ken it was Bob James at your front door and how did ye ken his name?'

'Charles told me that he'd researched your agency prior to coming to see you. Your photos are on your website. He continued to keep me informed, especially once he'd started to break down mentally again.'

'Aye right,' said Tracey, hoping Jo wouldn't guess the negative implications of the Scottish double positive and thinking that if Bertie had been here at this moment he too would have the makings of Mrs Jo Molesworth.

#

By the time Bob walked Sandra back to her car on Queen Charlotte Street and got back to the office, Tracey was long gone. Bertie looked around her desk and sniffed at the bin for leftover sausage roll before looking up at Bob to ask where his master had gone.

'No worries Bertie, I'll get it sorted. Oh, and thanks for your help at Molesworth's, that information you gave us may turn out to be paramount in this case.' It was then he noticed the pages of notes on the desk.

After reading them he phoned Tracey for a verbal translation before asking if it was okay for Bertie to stay the night at Rebecca's. Then he phoned Rebecca.

'Hi darling, sorry I've not had time to phone today.'

No answer.

'It's just we've had someone helping us with the Molesworth case this afternoon and I was telling him all about the way you cook a sirloin. He's asked if he can come for tea. You might be very interested to hear what he has to say.' He waited.

'Dinner won't be till seven. Sophie and I will have to prepare.'

'Listen, don't go to any trouble. I'm sure he won't mind at such short notice.'

'See you at seven Bob!'

Bob put the phone in his jacket pocket and looked down at Bertie, who's tail was wagging even harder.

CHAPTER EIGHT

Friday 19th June

Bertie turned out to be the perfect visitor the night before, having immediately taken Sophie and the sirloin to his heart. The feeling was mutual as far as Sophie was concerned, causing Bob to think a wee canine friend an ideal Christmas gift for her. The same couldn't be said for her mother though, the love of dogs not one of hers. It took all of Bob's ingenuity to come up with a rescue plan, which he put into place just after dinner.

His invitation for her to escort him on a return visit to Willie Dewar's house did lighten the atmosphere enough for them to be able to enjoy what was left of the evening.

Rebecca was looking out of the window of the Volvo as it sped past the sandstone piles on Gamekeepers Road. 'I knew exactly what you were doing last night, inviting me to come with you today.'

'Good, I really need you with me; your people skills might just sway the conversation enough to have Willie Dewar open up about Molesworth.'

'Those skills certainly didn't sway the conversation over dinner last night.'

'Maybe you've not got it where dogs are concerned. I thought you'd enjoy having Bertie to stay; Sophie certainly seemed to.'

She didn't bother to grace him with an answer but continued looking out from the car window.

'I think you'll find Willie Dewar an interesting character.'

'Bertie doesn't like me.'

'Of course he does.'

'And you really shocked me when you told me about Sandra.'

'She shocked me too. As I said, she really hasn't been herself lately and no bloody wonder.'

Rebecca turned from the window to look straight at him. 'I had a cancer scare once. It was awful'

'You never said.'

'It was years ago. It turned out to be a cyst, it was benign and removed. I did have to attend afterwards just to be sure. I was so worried and Sandra will be too, though she may not say so.'

'Did you attend the Maggie Centre at the Western General?'

'It was the Murrayfield at first then I was sent to the Maggie Centre.'

'Of course.'

'What do you mean, "of course"? No don't bother to answer that. It's just another slight at my having money. My family could afford private health care and that saved the NHS money but it took the resources of the NHS to make sure I was okay. My family had paid, along with everyone else, into the NHS. Isn't it time you got over it Bobby? Ever since we met you have continued with your rich girl, poor boy routine. First you tried to get me to dress down for your colleagues and that has continued since. I'm beginning to feel like the girl with the diamonds on the souls of her shoes.'

Bob resisted the temptation to agree with her last statement. 'Listen, Beccy, I'm sorry, I've a lot on my mind at the moment.'

'Well might I suggest you take some weight off that mind by forgetting about my money! It might help you concentrate on the case. Have you told Sandra yet, you know about the Molesworth visit?'

He decided not to grace this last question with a reply.

'You'd better tell me about Willie Dewar before we get there?'

He was relieved when the subject turned to the job in hand. 'Not a lot to tell really. Willie comes from a successful fishing family. They had their own deep-sea trawlers sailing out of Granton and employed quite a few men from the area. According to Willie they were sold down the proverbial by the UK Government. That was when he started the charity for the fishermen who no longer had work or the transferable skills to move to other employment. Unemployment benefit was much to be desired in those days and the charity helped a great many either retrain or retire more comfortably than otherwise would have been possible.'

'He sounds like a good egg.'

'That's what I believed, but what happened to his charity at the hands of Charles Molesworth left much to be desired and it might have caused him to do things he might now regret. When you meet him he comes across as hale fellow well met, but he's not the type you'd want to cross. He's been a hard man in his day; he'd have had to be to be a skipper of a deep-sea trawler.'

'And you think he's capable of causing Molesworth's death?'

'I just don't know.'

'What about his board members?'

'His what?'

'He couldn't run a charity without trust members. Your partner Tod would have known all about that in his job as a Community Worker.'

'Come to think about it he banged on about that quite a bit.'

'We'll need to interview them too so we'd better get their names and contact details.'

'Right boss.'

'That's better.' Rebecca smiled for the first time that morning.

#

It didn't take them long to reach Blackhall and Willie Dewar's bungalow. Rebecca pointed to a BMW sports car sitting directly outside the house. Don't tell me Mr Dewar drives that. He must be well off; it's the type of car one would expect your DS Mackay to drive. How is he by the way?'

'You're about to find out. It's his car. He's waiting for us inside.'

'What?'

'Sandra asked me to take him under my wing in her absence.'

'You bastard! You played me along, the little girl lost. You don't need me here Bob James!'

'Now Beccy, calm down. I do need you here, that's the truth. I was afraid if I told you John would be here too that you might renege.'

'Well I just have. And don't worry, I can get a taxi home, after all I can afford it.'

As she was about to open the car door, John Mackay appeared and opened it for her. 'Rebecca, good to see you, haven't seen you since the Gormand case. How are you?'

Bob couldn't work out if it was John's verbal charm or his good looks that caused her to relax. 'Oh, I'm fine John, thank you.'

'It's good to have you on board with this. DI Laing has given me the lead on the case; having you around will help a lot.'

She smiled and stepped down from the Volvo and pointed to the BMW. 'I like the car. Are you still rallying?'

'I am. In fact, I'm racing tomorrow, or was, but my co-driver has taken ill.'

Cold feet more like, thought Bob, having seen how John could handle a motor.

'You wouldn't fancy coming on board would you? It's a male/female event.'

'Are you serious John?'

‘I couldn’t be more so. You’ll have to brush up on the course; I’ll email you the details and pick you up tomorrow morning at five. The race is near Moffat and starts at nine. If you’re up for staying on there’s a meal after, compliments of the circuit?’

Bob stared out through the windscreen, saying nothing. He’d asked John to help get her on side but hadn’t expected a sweetener as potent as this.

‘I would absolutely love to join you. Will we be staying over after the meal?’

John glanced at Bob just as Bob turned to face him. ‘I don’t think so, the hotels are full.’

‘Oh, that is a pity,’ answered Rebecca. ‘Maybe next time.’

#

The office phone hadn’t rung much and when it did Tracey jumped slightly. She was sitting at her desk and searching the computer for everything she could find on the Fishermens Union, Charles Molesworth Solicitors and Jo Molesworth. She looked at the phone screen but didn’t recognise the number. Scam call she was thinking but answered regardless.

‘JP Associates, Tracey Cowan investigator speaking.’

‘My you’ve certainly come up in the world.’

‘Tod?’

‘We’re allowed to make calls you know, especially when one is a friend of Jimmy McGuire.’

‘To what dae A owe the pleasure?’

‘That’s more like it. Is Bob there?’

‘No, he’s on the Molesworth job.’

‘Good, it’s you I wanted to speak to. How do you think our twelve literacy learners are getting on?’

‘What a daft question. We’ve only been doing it for two weeks; a wee bit soon for an evaluation, don’t ye think?’

‘I just wondered.’

'They're getting on great.'

'How do you know?'

'Jimmy told me. They think you're the best thing since sliced bread.'

'That's thanks to you Tracey, not me.'

'Aye, so it is. Ye dinnae need tae butter me up, A'm happy daen it.'

'Maybe you should think about being a full-time literacy tutor?'

'A've got a job thanks. Are you trying to get rid of me by any chance?'

'Now, now. How's Bertie?'

'He's fine. He stayed out last night at Rebecca's.'

'Don't tell me Bob's taken a shine to him.'

'Mair than a shine, A think he's trying tae steal him. A didnae even ken he liked dogs.'

'He was interested in becoming a dog handler with the police when he was a young constable, but promotion came his way and that put paid to that.'

'Excuse me for asking, but is this just a social call boss?'

'Someone has been to see me and I think you should know about it.'

'And whae might that be?'

'Daniel Manning.'

'Aw dinnae tell me, the spy whae came in fae the cauld. What is it this time?'

'He was here to warn me about the Molesworth case and he wanted to know what I know, which is very little, and I told him so.'

'Ye couldnae make this up. Is his boss still wanting tae protect his darling niece Rebecca from us bad lot in Leith?'

'No, it's worse than that.'

'What?'

‘He wants us to drop the case and we may have to.’

‘Why?’

‘MI6 were heavily involved in the Bosnian war and were in attendance at the trials in the Hague, albeit clandestinely. They were carrying out activities in Bosnia that should never see the light of day. They followed this up at the trials to make sure everyone involved was silent, or silenced. According to Daniel, the Molesworth case has raised the subject once more. He told me that Peter had been heavily involved in the Bosnian conflict and that Molesworth’s witness would have raised some very serious issues for MI6 at the trials, had she not died in the accident.’

Tracey remembered what Jo Molesworth had told her about the girl in the Hague, and her being killed. The idea entered her head that it could have been the Security Services who were haunting Molesworth. ‘Does Bob know anything about your visit from Daniel?’

‘Not yet, not as far as I know, but Bob visited Daniel at his pitch in Waverley Station. Tracey, have you spoken with Callum Mackie?’

‘Aye, I was asking him about poltergeists.’

‘Shit.’

‘What’s wrong wie that, he is a church minister.’

‘Yes, and he’s also a retired SBS operative who worked with Peter in Bosnia.’

‘Shit.’

‘Exactly. Please be careful Tracey, I really do believe JP Associates has bitten of more than it can chew this time.’

‘Is that why you want me out of it?’

‘Maybe.’

‘Sorry A cannae oblige. It will take mair than Uncle Peter and his motley crew tae scare me.’

He’d hung up before hearing her last words.

#

Willie Dewar stood in the bay window of his bungalow watching the goings-on between the three visitors. He looked down across his front garden. The gnomes he'd been making since retiring from fishing crowded every space. There were trawlers too and a pottery model of Granton Harbour as it used to be.

He was most proud of the fishermen gnomes; the crews that had manned his boats. He smiled to himself as he looked at Molesworth and wondered how long it would be before his visitors would end up part of his collection.

CHAPTER NINE

Saturday 20th June

Bob rose early to see Rebecca off on her trip to Moffat with John. He'd parked his Land Rover on the street as her drive would not have accommodated the long trailer carrying a very sporty looking rally car.

'Don't wait up darling,' she called, as she rushed out of the gate, hardly bothering to turn around.

Bob didn't walk back into the house, choosing instead to go to the end of Gamekeepers Road and down Peggy's Mill Road to the River Almond.

It was still only five-thirty and there was not a soul around. The only sounds came from the morning chorus of birds in the tall trees and the cascading water of the green river as it flowed towards the Firth of Forth.

He'd not been able to get Sandra off his mind since she'd told him of her cancer. The two of them went back a long way, back as far as their training at Tulliallan. He had great respect for Sandra. Some believed that respect was actually a crush and maybe it was, once upon a time, before he found out that she was gay. Unrequited love indeed.

When he got to the river's edge he stopped and looked across at the trees on the other bank. Dalmeny Estate, another rich pile for the Earls Roseberry, another rich family, another world. I'm getting more like Tod, he thought, as he turned southward towards Cramond Brig.

His thoughts jumped back to Willie Dewar and those gnomes. Certainly good with his hands but what a memorial. Everyone and everything he'd known, presented in clay for the world to see. The people they represented were mostly dead. It hadn't taken him long to stick Molesworth in there either, pride and place in the centre of it all. Some hobby.

He was contemplating that perhaps another visit to Willie was in order when his mobile rang. He took it quickly from his pocket, not wishing to disturb early morning Cramond and hoping that it might be Rebecca. 'Yes?'

'It's me Bob, Tracey.'

'So it is. It's just passed six in the morning and it's a Saturday. Are you looking for overtime?'

'Tod called me yesterday and it's something you need tae hear.'

'What, at this time in the morning?'

'I've been up half the night thinking about it. Tod didn't want you to know about the call. He phoned me because he's worried about me.'

'And I wouldn't be?'

'We'll need tae meet, are ye at hame?'

'No. I'm having a walk at the Almond.'

'That's early. Is Rebecca with you?'

'No, she's away rallying with John Mackay.'

'Mm. I'll come tae Rebecca's. Harry knows nothing about this either.

'Forget Rebecca's, I'll get back to the car and meet you at the hotel at Crew Toll. What's it called?'

'The Village.'

'Right. I'll see you there at eight. I'm on the breakfast.'

'That's a first.'

'Play your cards right and it might not be your last.'

#

By the time John and Rebecca had reached Leadburn and the right turn that would take them to Moffat, he'd been made well aware of Rebecca's feelings for Bob, which pleased him no end. She'd hardly stopped speaking about his ex-DI since she'd got in the car and in her own subtle way was making it clear she was unavailable.

Not that he needed to know that of course as he already had a partner. Nigel worked in finance and it was he, more than John's own wealthy family, who helped finance his ventures into the world of racing.

#

'What did Harry say about you leaving the house so early?'

'Not much; he's a wee bit hungover. Mrs Spale put on a wee spread for the staff last night and she couldnae dae that without ma Harry taking pride of place.'

'You're a bit jealous of Evelyn Spale eh.'

'Me? No. It just makes me feel a bit sick tae see him drooling all over her.'

'He loves you to bits Tracey.'

'Aye, and Rebecca loves you too Bob. Maybe you should cut her some slack.'

'Cut her some slack, you've been watching to many American movies. We better help ourselves to the buffet breakfast before you tell me all about Tod's phone call.'

Once they were seated again and Tracey had recovered from seeing the amount of food on Bob's plate she spelled out in detail Tod's warning.

For one moment she thought Tod's information had put her boss off his breakfast, particularly when he slid the plate away from him and put his large hands flat on the table. 'You couldn't make this up if you tried.'

‘Yep, you’ve said it we’ve got ourselves involved in another conspiracy. Talking about conspiracies, you didnae tell me ye’d been tae see Daniel Manning. What was that about?’

He pulled his plate back towards him. ‘Oh that? I wanted to ask if he could help with our stalker.’

‘Well at least A was right about one thing; this case involves mair spooks than meets the eye.’

CHAPTER TEN

Sunday 21st June

Sunday visiting was as busy as Bob had expected when he arrived at the prison. But he'd phone ahead and made sure that Tod did not have any other visitors booked in.

Rebecca had declined his invitation to join him on the pretext that she was exhausted after her rallying experience. Bob suspected it might be more to do with a fear of prisons but couldn't be sure.

Once he'd left the house he called Valerie and asked if she would like to pay Tod a visit. From the silence at the other end of the phone he thought she was going to decline so when the answer came back, "yes, alright", he got quite a shock.

He didn't know Valerie well and was nervous as he waited for her at Newhaven Harbour. The second she got in the car he realised he needn't have been.

'Nice car.'

'A retirement present to myself.'

'Always fancied a Volvo but the works van will have to suffice till I can get that son of mine through Aberdeen Uni.'

'Tod told me your son was at uni and all about your job with the Government.'

'He told me all about you when he phoned last night. So let's just say I wasn't overly surprised when you phoned earlier.'

'You've not been to see him.' Although driving Bob turned to look at her.

‘No.’

‘Why not?’

‘I’m not sure.’

Did you know he was working for the Security Services?’

‘Before I confide in you maybe you should put your eyes back on the road.’

Bob swerved to avoid a cyclist. ‘The worst things on the road,’ he uttered.

‘Yes, I did know. He told me not long after we met actually.’

‘So, when we were in Cambridge, you knew then?’

‘That’s when he told me all about being recruited there. Do you have the painting hanging that I did for you when we were down there?’

‘As a matter of fact, I do. It still unnerves me though to think of my ancestor leaving that small village and coming to Edinburgh.’

‘People have moved across countries for millennia and for all sorts of reasons. I work with quite a few people who still get classed as foreigners.’

Bob parked in a tight space in the prison carpark, making it difficult for her to get out of the car.

‘I wonder if this is how it feels in prison?’ she said, as she tried to squeeze through the tight space.

#

They waited their turn in the queue and when their time came a warden escorted them to the visitors’ room. ‘Nice tae see ye again Bob,’ said the warden. You retired yet?’

‘I have that Bert. How’s things?’

‘Same old, same old. A wee bit political correctness creeping in though. Thank God I’ve only got another six months.’ Bert said this as if he were a prisoner. ‘Your Pal’s been getting a visitor or two lately.’

‘So I’ve heard.’

‘He seems tae have settled in quite well.’

‘Thanks to those who shall remain nameless eh.’

‘Aye. Ye heard then?

‘Come on Bert, it’s Bob James you’re talking to.’

As they reached the visitors’ room Bert took his leave.

‘He seemed to know you well enough,’ said Valerie, looking around the room.

He saw her fix her eyes on Tod who was sitting at a table at the far end of the room with his head down. Bob touched her shoulder ‘Well, are you not going to say hello?’

She made her way around the other tables and visitors, some who were laughing and some who were in tears. It wasn’t until she put her hand on his table that Tod looked up. When she saw his face, she joined in with the other visitors, those that were in tears.

He stood, leaned over and put his hand on her arm but didn’t speak.

When she did, it wasn’t what he was expecting. ‘Tracey told me you’re thinking about writing that book. What was it, Lullaby of the Soul?’

‘Is that why you’re crying?’

‘Of course, I’ve seen your writing Dougal.’

He laughed out loud for the first time in a very long time.

Bob was smiling as he walked towards them, aware that he’d underestimated Valerie Napier. It was just then he spotted Jimmy McGuire sitting with who he took to be one of his sons. He changed direction.

‘Aw Son, wid ye look what the cat’s dragged in,’ said Jimmy. ‘If it isnae the great and the good Bob James.’

Jimmy’s son turned around and looked up at Bob.

'Aye that's right son,' said Bob, 'I just can't stay away from the likes of your Dad. Has he been teaching you the ways of our Lord, or are you planning another heist Jimmy?'

'Malcolm, this is the famous Detective Inspector Bob James, recently retired fae Scotland's finest. Before A found a different path he and I had a close working relationship, isn't that right Bob.'

Before he could answer Jimmy's son stood up. He was taller and broader than Bob and looked him straight in the eye.

'Now, I wouldn't think of doing anything silly son,' said Bob.

'A was just going tae offer ye ma seat.'

'No thanks, I'll stand if you don't mind. I only wanted to say hello to your Dad.'

'Well you've said your hello, so why don't you sling your hook over tae your tart.'

Just as he said this he collapsed on the floor. Bob stepped back, arms apart to indicate he'd not touched him. Jimmy looked up at Bob, smiled and winked, giving his old adversary the excuse to turn and walk over to join Tod and Valerie.

'I saw that,' said Valerie. 'That old man kicked him on the back of the knee. What did he do that for?'

'I've no idea. It's maybe some form of direct parenting skills.' answered Bob, taking a seat beside her . 'Good afternoon partner.'

'Hi Bob. What brings you here on this lovely afternoon?'

'Tracey told me about your phone call.'

'I was concerned after what Daniel told me.'

'If what you told her is true even Bertie will not be able to save her. It was you who gave her the dog, am I right?'

'No.'

'Who was it?'

'Callum. He believed we weren't giving her enough attention and wanted to let her know, in his own indubitable fashion, that she was indispensable to our agency.'

'Harry bought her a deerstalker which she insists on wearing.'

It was Valerie's turn to laugh out loud.

'So what is this stuff with Daniel all about? I've already been to see him at the station so he now knows about the stalker and will have put two and two together.'

'He told me everything that had gone on in Bosnia involving the Security Services. Peter Blue was there, as was Callum Mackie and Daniel. Things went on that shouldn't have. Things that cannot come to light, no matter what. He didn't say outright but it's a political hot potato. It's quite likely that Mr Molesworth met his end because of what he knew about it. Either way, we can't be involved and need to call a halt.'

'That's all very well, but what if it wasn't the Security Service that killed Molesworth but a different kind of spook? We've got another two possible suspects under investigation. There's Willie Dewar who manages the Fishermens Union; Molesworth nearly bankrupt it, and Willie. Then there's Molesworth's wife, I'm not sure about her at all. Mind you, our resident stalker does point to Security Service involvement.'

'This is all a matter of conjecture and a matter for the police is it not? I don't think Sandra would be very happy to know we were doing their work for them again, do you? Oh and for the record I told Daniel about the problems at Spale and Co.'

'Oh Tod, what in Heaven's name?

'They need his help.'

'Aye, maybe they do? Sandra knows we're involved with the Molesworth case. It was her that asked for my help. I've been reemployed on a consultancy basis again and told to work with MIT and Sandra.' It suddenly dawned on Bob as he was speaking that the reason he may have been taken on was that the Chief may already have known about Sandra's ill-health.

'Margaret Whalen may not be too happy about that?'

'She has got herself a new boss, DI Sammy Brogue. He's alright. Margaret and Sandra are no longer an item and Sandra is still using my gaff at the moment. Of course, you'll know all this from Tracey at your Wednesday night classes.'

'Tracey doesn't divulge anything during the class. There's no time.'

'So you don't know about Sandra's cancer?'

'No.'

'She's having tests.'

'Poor woman,' said Valerie, her interruption reminding them both that she was a visitor too.

'I'm sorry Val,' said Tod, 'about Sandra too.'

'Aye, sorry Valerie,' added Bob. 'I'm just not sure where we go with this now.'

'What about Mark?' she asked.

'What about him? He's working for Callum now.'

'Exactly. Could we not get Mark to subtly question him about his time in Bosnia? After all Dr le Mot does have a psychology degree.'

'And how do you propose that Mark raises that subject?' asked Bob.

'I think I may know a way.'

'And what might that be?' asked Tod.

Valerie winked at him as she stood up. 'That's for me to know and you to find out Dougal.'

#

As they were driving north to Newhaven Bob raised the subject of her calling Tod, Dougal.

‘You’ll have to read Muriel Spark’s Ballad of Peckham Rye. You’ll get the drift then,’ was all she said in reply.

CHAPTER ELEVEN

Friday 26th June

Callum and Mark had just said their goodbyes to the other delegates at the drug rehabilitation conference in London when they both received a text from Valerie. She would like them both to join her for supper at her house in Newhaven that evening. After a short discussion they both replied with thanks.

Their conversation on the train was taken up by their success at the conference. The offers of support from other projects left them feeling high spirited indeed.

Having left London at 7am they were in Edinburgh by lunchtime and intended to spend the rest of the day in the office in Leith.

Callum remained somewhat intrigued by Valerie's invitation and thought that it must have something to do with their earlier meeting by the Water of Leith.

When they arrived at their centre they were surprised to find a youngish woman of African descent waiting for them. She didn't look as if she was there for help with a drug problem though they soon discovered, even before entering the building, that she was.

Once inside and seated in Callum's office she explained in full why she had found her way to BEYOND. Her request was for the agency to help her with something that bothered her greatly. It was not something either of them had given much thought to, though they'd seen that more than one of the stalls at the conference in

London highlighted the subject; neither of them thought to attend those stalls.

'Methadone,' said Mark, 'is not really something we have given much thought too Daniella?'

'I assume then that your programme focuses on other methodologies?' She held up her fingers to indicate inverted commas when she said the word "methodologies".

'We do work closely with other projects and have been in discussions with BETHANY and others,' answered Callum.

'Yes, but what about your project? How many clients do you have for example?'

'It's early days. We only fully began the project in May.'

'I see. Why did you call it BEYOND?'

'That was Mark's idea. Mark, would you like to explain to Daniella where that idea came from.'

'Certainly. It stems from a quote of Arthur C. Clarke's work. He believed that the only way of finding the limits of the possible is by going "beyond" them to the impossible.' I prefer to think of it as the direction we hope our clients will go.' Mark leaned back in his chair rather pleased with his response.

'So what you are saying is that methadone users can go beyond the possible by reaching into the impossible?'

'Not in so many words, but that is the general idea.' He took a large sip of his coffee.

'This is very interesting Dr le Mot and something I would like to talk with you at length about. Do you have any writings on the subject that I can give to my clients, or leaflets on your courses perhaps? I'm sure many of them would be very interested in making that journey.'

Mark stood, went to his desk drawer and took out a pile of leaflet. 'We've not had a chance to hand them out yet.'.

'That's okay, I will be doing that starting tomorrow.'

‘Well if we are done for the day,’ said Callum, standing. ‘So where is it you are from exactly Daniella?’

‘Oh, I live locally, North Fort Street. My pharmacy is in Ferry Road. What about yourself Reverend Mackie?’

Callum smiled broadly, as did Daniella.

‘I think we are going to get on very well, don’t you?’ she said to them both as she walked to the door.

‘So, whose idea was it to come back to the office?’ said Mark, when she’d gone.

‘I was just thinking that myself Mark. Do I look so much like a minister of the kirk?

‘Maybe.’

‘Aye, maybe. Our Daniella doesn’t appear to be lacking in intellectual understanding, does she?’

‘Are you referring to the name?’

‘No, not specifically. But even you must admit that BEYOND is somewhat esoteric.’

‘And what’s wrong with that.’

‘Nothing much, but where Daniella and drug rehabilitation is concerned, I think we may have just sown the wind and will shortly reap the whirlwind. Anyway, enough of that. It’s still early and we’re not due at Valerie’s till seven-thirty. I thought you might fancy a wee aperitif.’

Mark’s face lit up, for the first time that afternoon.

#

Bob had spent the week trying to get in touch with Peter Blue. He’d tried both his, and Sean’s phone and had twice gone to the house in Northumberland Street but no answer.

Rebecca was no help either and hadn’t heard from her uncle Peter in weeks. That left Bob with no option but to spend the week going between JP’s office on Great Junction Street, Fettes Command Centre and his own flat in Portobello, where he took it upon himself to inform Sandra of the goings-on with the Security Services.

He thought he might get his head in his hands but it was the opposite, she merely said that she'd welcome any distraction from her pending diagnosis.

She also thought that a picnic for her, Bob and Tracey on Portobello Prom might be a good idea and it was arranged for the Friday. They agreed to meet just outside the swimming baths on the prom.

On their way from the office Bob stopped at Greggs in Portobello and waited on the double yellow lines while Tracey bought a variety of goodies for the picnic.

When they got to the prom, Sandra was already there, sitting on the sea wall. 'I see you've brought the JP lunch of choice.'

'Nothing but the best for DI Sandra Laing, eh Tracey,' replied Bob.

'Is Tracey the company message lassie as well as secretary and investigator?'

Bob didn't answer but sat down beside her on the wall.

'It's a pity Big Jake wasn't here to help enjoy this, I believe it was his choice of fayre too.' Sandra looked at Tracey as she said this.

'Aye it was.' She put the bag against the wall between the two ex-colleagues and looked out to sea.

'You miss him Tracey,' said Sandra.'

'Aye.'

'I miss the big bugger too,' added Bob.

'I didn't get to know him as much as I'd have liked. They say he was worth getting to know though. Rumour had it in Fettes that he was the mastermind behind JP Associates success.'

'They called him the Oracle.' Tracey turned to face them as they looked into the Greggs bag. He used to say he had a finger in every pie and I can see you two are the same. I'd better delve in before they're polished off.' She put her hand into the bag of warm food.

'What do you make of all this stuff about Molesworth and the Security Services Tracey?'

'A might have not have believed it if it wisnae Daniel Manning who'd contacted Tod. He was, and might still be an operative with MI5. He's friendly with Tod.' She thought for a moment. 'A believe it.'

'Where does that leave us with Willie Dewar and Molesworth's wife Jo? Does that take them out the frame?'

'I hope you don't mind me interrupting Sandra,' said Bob. 'In case you sleuths are forgetting, this is my case.'

Sandra turned to look at him. 'Since when? Wasn't it me who asked you to accompany me to Molesworth's. This is a Police Scotland case, or was until your friend Tod Peterson got involved and brought the Security Services along for good measure.'

As if on cue, Bob's mobile rang. When he saw who it was he stood and walked away before answering. 'Beccy.'

'I've been in touch with Uncle Peter.'

'How did you manage that?'

'With great diligence and perseverance. Plus, I got fed-up listening to your griping every evening.'

'You really are a sweetheart.'

'That's what they all say. See you tonight at seven sharp remember. And don't be late or the rack of lamb may be overdone.'

'When am I seeing Peter?

Uncle Peter is coming here mid-morning tomorrow. Oh and Bobby, it's we who are seeing him.'

He smiled as he put his phone in his jacket pocket.

'You look a happy bunny,' said Sandra.

'So would you if you'd just been told it was rack of lamb for dinner.'

'Dinner?' asked Tracey. A thought ye called it your tea, or was that when ye lived in Granton?'

'Gamekeepers Road's maybe getting to him Tracey.'

'That's what A was thinking.'

#

Callum and Mark didn't overstay their welcome in the Shore bar and arrived at Valerie's exactly on time. As they were waiting for the lift Callum began fiddling in his jacket pocket.

'You seem nervous Callum, are you alright?'

'Aye.'

'It's just you have been in and out of your jacket pocket since we left the bar.'

Callum thought for a moment before producing a small red box from the pocket in question and opening it. 'I got this for Valerie when we were in London.'

'A St. Christopher. Not seen one of those in a while. I thought he'd gone out of fashion with the public as well as the church.'

'Not with me though. I thought she might like to wear it on her travels around Scotland. I wanted to cheer her up after our last meeting.'

'Is that not a bit over the top? We hardly know her.'

'Valerie and I go back a long way son.'

'Son, you've never called me that before.'

'Old habits die hard, sorry.'

'And is Valerie an old habit?'

'No, not in the way you're thinking. I met her a time or two a few years ago. As a matter of fact, I own two of her works.'

'Really. How did that come about?'

'Why do I get the feeling I am being subjected to psychological scrutiny here Doctor le Mot?'

Mark laughed out loud and asked no more.

As they stepped from the lift on Valerie's floor she was there to greet them. 'Now that's what I call punctual.'

'Do you always await your visitors in the hallway?' asked Callum.

'Only the special ones get that privilege. I saw you getting out the taxi just by Asda. They do lovely flowers, for a supermarket.'

Her remark immediately drew the men's attention to that fact that they hadn't bothered to bring any. 'Oh sorry,' they said in unison.

'It's lucky for you I'm a twenty-first century girl and couldn't possibly accept such frivolities from my male callers. You'd better come in, tea's about ready.'

They could smell what awaited them before they'd crossed the threshold. 'Is that Cullen Skink I smell?' asked Mark.

'You've got a nose on you le Mot. I thought some Mediterranean olives with garlic flat bread to start though, followed by the Cullen Skink We've the most wonderful fishmonger here at the harbour. You do like fish I hope? And I thought we'd finish off with some French cheeses and Scottish handmade oatcakes.'

Mark was almost salivating as she showed them into the living-room. A set dining table took centre place in the middle of the small room. Mark walked to the window. 'What a view. I remember that scene from your painting that hung in JP's office.'

Callum appeared to be ignoring Mark and was looking at the paintings that were hanging all around the room.

'Do you like them Callum?' asked Valerie as she placed a large bowl of olives and the garlic bread on the table.

'Quite different,' he answered. 'Is this from a new exhibition?'

'Yes mostly, but some of the work's not mine. One or two have been painted by my students. On my field trips around the Highlands I have met some very interesting people.'

Callum continued scanning the walls, until his eye caught a particular piece. He stared for some moments until Valerie interrupted his train of thought.

'Do you like it?'

He didn't answer but continued staring.

'Well?'

'That's not the Highlands of Scotland.'

'No. Do you recognise were it is?'

'I'm not sure.'

'You've been there. Or so Tod says.'

'Have you been to see him?'

'Yes. Bob drove me to the prison. What about the painting?'

'Have you been to Bosnia?'

'No, but one of the families I work with in Ullapool are from Bosnia, and their daughter painted this. That's her as a fourteen-year-old standing by that gate with the ruins all around her. I found it so moving and bought it from her. Those ruined cottages and wrecked farms. In a way it reminded me of what it must have been like in Scotland after Culloden.'

'Callum began to look unsteady on his feet.

'Are you alright Callum, you look like you've seen a ghost.'

'I'm not sure. Look, I'm really sorry but I think I'm going to have to go. It might be something I ate on the train on the way back from London. Mark will do your cooking justice.'

Mark turned from the window just as Callum was leaving the room. 'Is this the window that you painted the harbour from in the painting that hung in JP's office, the one with the fishing boat?'

'It is.'

It's a great view. Is Callum off to the loo?'

'No, he's not feeling too good and gave his apologies. I'm not sure what's wrong but he seems to think it might have been food poisoning from the food on the train.'

'That's odd, we only had a biscuit with our coffee. We'd had breakfast in the hotel.'

'Och well he's maybe picked up a wee bug. But we can't let all this food go to waste, can we Mark?'

For a moment he was in two minds whether to follow his boss, until his eyes caught the bowl of olives. 'I suppose not.'

'Don't worry, he'll be fine by morning. I know where he lives and will check on him. Now you get your jacket off and get tucked in Dr le Mot.'

CHAPTER TWELVE

Saturday 27th June

When Bob woke the light that would normally be bathing his Gamekeepers Road bedroom was nonexistent and he was in darkness. He stumbled onto the floor and turned to see if Rebecca was still in bed but when he saw the empty bed he realised that he was in his own house. That's when the memory that remained of yesterday began falling into place.

After the picnic he and Sandra had decided on a drink. Tracey emphatically reneged, so they got her a taxi and told her to take what was left of the afternoon off.

Bob couldn't quite remember what time they'd left the pub but did remember walking up the road with Sandra at his side and them both tucking into fish suppers.

When he stumbled through to the kitchen Sandra was already up and dressed and looking no worse for their sojourns. 'You'd better get yourself moving or Rebecca will not be well pleased.'

'Aye. I'm seeing her uncle this morning.'

'Do you not remember you told me that last night.'

'Oh aye, so I did.'

'And that's not all you told me.'

'What else?'

'About your phobia with ghosts. You asked if I was scared of them.'

'I must have been pished. And what did you say?'

'No. You even asked if it could have been a ghost that killed Molesworth.'

'I must have been well on.'

'Aye, you were. But worse, you were serious. You really do have a phobia. You might need hypnotherapy. I know a good lad who works in the Scottish Borders.'

'A good what? Never mind, I'll have a worse problem if I don't get my arse in gear and get to Beccy's.'

'I'm coming with you.'

'There's no need for that Sandra. I don't need you to hold my hand.'

'No, but you need me to drive. You're well over the limit.'

'You didn't try to take advantage of me did you?'

'Chance would be a fine thing says you. Now go and get yourself tidied up, we've a spook to meet.'

#

Valerie arrived at Callum's at ten o'clock and rang the bell hard repeatedly until he opened the door.

'Val, Valerie, what in Heaven's name are you doing here at this time on a Saturday morning?'

'Is that blaspheming?'

'What?'

'Evoking Heaven in a greeting.'

'Come away in and put the kettle on. And Val, you shouldn't be listening to Tracey so much; Heaven is a case of perspective. You make the tea, I'll get out of this dressing gown now there's a lady present.'

When he returned he was in his old tracksuit, the one with the Special Boat Service badge on the trousers. Valerie was sitting at the kitchen table mug in hand.

'I see you found the biscuit barrel. If I'd known you were coming I'd have baked a cake.'

‘How are you feeling this morning?’

‘It must have been indigestion, I’m feeling lots better thanks. And sorry about last night.’

‘Yes, you did leave in an awful hurry. Mark was worried about you, well until I presented the food.’ At that Valerie hoisted her bag onto the table and lifted out three containers. ‘Your leftovers. What really went wrong last night Callum?’

‘The painting of that village in Bosnia.’

‘Why should that have upset you so much?’

‘It’s a long story.’

‘I’ve got all morning.’

#

As Callum was divulging, under duress, what really went on with the Security Services in Bosnia, Harry Cowan was being subjected to his own interrogation.

‘A still dinnae understand why you have tae go tae aw those drink parties wie Mrs Spale?’

‘Tracey, A’ve told ye umpteen times, Evelyn has not long lost her man and she’s trying her best to manage the business and the mess that Philip Gormand left behind. She’s a woman on her own remember.’

‘So am A, well that’s how it feels. She only has tae call and off ye go; yes Mrs Spale, no Mrs Spale. We were supposed tae be having a night at the tellie last night but you roll in after nine, half pished, telling me yer gaun tae yer bed cause ye’ve had a hard week. Well A’m not having it, not for Mrs Spale or anybody so ye can ring her up the day and tell her your giving in yer notice.’

‘A cannae dae that darling.’

‘Well, if ye dinnae, A’m handing in mine. A’ve had enough of your philandering. It’s her or me Harry.’

#

Rebecca was surprised to see Sandra's car draw into the drive, but that was only until she saw Bob stagger slightly as he got out. She got to the front door before they could ring the bell.

'Thanks for last night's warning Inspector Laing, or I may not have recognised Mr James. Rather the worse for wear are we darling?'

Bob had no idea that Sandra had phoned Rebecca to tell her that he wouldn't be home. He turned to Rebecca 'Not on your life sweetheart, but I could murder a coffee.'

'Sophie has the cheese scones ready to go in the oven. Uncle Peter should be here anytime soon,'

Bob was pleasantly surprised at his warm reception but thought it had more to do with Sandra's intervention and less to do with his charm, abundant or otherwise. 'I don't suppose that Peter and I could meet privately?'

'No!' came the reply in unison from Rebecca and Sandra.

The echo of their emphatic "No" had hardly cleared from his ears when they heard the sound of a car on the gravel drive. Rebecca walked over to the bay window. She rushed to the front door. 'That's him now.'

'I hope you don't mind Rebecca, but I've brought my man with me. The ex-Irish Guardsman nodded to her. 'Shaun does all my driving now and I knew you wouldn't want him left out here in the cold.'

Aye right, thought Bob, the spy who came in from the cold right enough.

'Good morning Bob, nice to see you again.'

'You too Peter. And you Shaun, it's been a while, indeed; forty-six days to be exact. How's the legs; are you back playing shinty yet?'

'Certainly not legless Bob and in better shape than Philip Gormand'

'Mm'

'How is your partner Thomas holding up? Be sure to tell him I'm asking for him on your next visit.'

'You'll be able to tell him soon enough yourself. From what I hear Security Service operators don't normally spend over long in prison.'

'Now, now gentlemen,' interjected Peter, before too much was said. He turned to Rebecca. 'Is that cheese scones I'm smelling darling?'

'It most certainly is Uncle and made by Sophie, especially for you.'

Bob couldn't quite work out whether it was the night before or their behaviour that was making him feel sick. 'Did you not say she'd made them for me?'

'I never said such a thing!'

Peter's smile got broader. 'How is Sophie? She'll be going off to Cambridge again soon no doubt.'

'She's decided to remain at home and has put in an application for a transfer to Edinburgh.'

'Good choice.' The conversation continued as they walked to the kitchen. 'Will she be taking the same subjects?'

'No, quite a change of direction. She's applied to study psychology.'

'Good for her,' said Peter, loudly enough for Sophie to hear. 'Isn't that young researcher, Mark le…something a psychology student?'

'Sophie rushed from the kitchen and put her arms around his waist. 'Uncle Peter, he's Doctor Mark le Mot now.'

'Dearest Sophie, your Mum tells me you'll not be going back to Cambridge and will be staying on in Edinburgh.'

'Yes Uncle.'

'Well isn't it just fitting that I moved up here too.'

Bob was becoming quite agitated by the performance and Sandra spotted it. 'Sophie, I've been hearing a lot about your cheese scones.'

'They're just out the oven. Come on, or they'll get cold.'

Bob began wondering how he'd manage to pay the bill for Sandra's life-saving gestures and chose a subtle wink as down payment.

Once familiarities were over and the scones and coffee devoured everyone retired to the conservatory. The offer of more coffee was refused by all and Bob managed not to request the hair of the dog. They took their seats and waited.

'I thought it best if we just cut to the chase regarding rumours that are going around regarding the recent death of Charles Molesworth. I can tell you quite categorically that his death had nothing what so ever to do with the Security Services. Despite the wild rumours that abound north of the border, particularly in Leith, the Service does not sanction murder.'

'What about Tod Uncle Peter?'

Please can I ask you not to interrupt Sophie, I will be open to questions at the end.'

What a smug bastard, thought Bob and Sandra, simultaneously.

'Everyone here seems to have created a link between the service and Mr Molesworth down to happenings in Bosnia, but the British contingent stationed there were part of a UN protection force. UK observers and liaison staff had been on the ground from early on in Sarajevo and elsewhere but only until the main force, the Cheshire Regiment arrived.'

'He was about to roll on until Bob spoke. 'Liaising with who?'

'Pardon?'

'You heard.' Bob could hear the others shuffle slightly in their chairs. 'Who were the liaison staff liaising with?'

'What a silly question. Leaders and politicians of course.'

‘Oh I see. What about militias?’ Did they liaise with paramilitary groups as a means to using them to do the killing work that the US preferred? After all, the UN peacekeeping fiasco got so many killed unnecessarily. Surely most commanders on the ground would have tried to find a way round that wee problem.’ Once again Bob could hear Tod’s voice talk through him.

‘I don’t know who is giving you this information Bob but it’s obviously fabricated. Now if I may continue. Britain’s main initial contribution to the UN was observing and liaison. This contribution to the UN initiative was based around 1st Battalion Cheshire Regiment. In 1992-1995 it took part primarily in Peacekeeping duties in Bosnia. In addition to protecting convoys one of its main tasks was to ensure freedom of movement within the Muslim-Croat Federation.

You’re very well versed in the history Peter but what was your role? Sorry, I’ll rephrase that. What was the role of MI6 in the peace-keeping duties? Everyone turned with surprise to look at Sandra, the one who’d asked the question.

Peter went red in the face, giving his man servant his cue. ‘From my limited knowledge of the conflict, what Colonel Blue says is accurate.’

“I think if Tod Peterson was here Sean, he might see Uncle Peter’s version as a fine use of verisimilitude.’ Said Sophie. ‘In y studies in Cambridge I did learn about its use. The appearance of truth I believe it means. For such a complex theatre of war, Uncle’s version seems somewhat simplified.

‘And how do you come to that conclusion darling?’ asked Uncle Peter.

My A-Levels. I chose Modern History and in particular the war in Bosnia.’

Bob thought Peter's eyes were about to pop out of his head. 'And what did your school master teach you that I have not yet covered?'

She had a reputation as a radical and she wanted us to look under the surface of events. For example, the tensions between the UK and America.

'I don't remember any tension.'

My teacher told us that British officials were worried that tensions between the UK and US over Bosnia-Herzegovina would poison the wider relationship between prime minister John Major and America's newly elected president Bill Clinton. Britain was for maintaining an arms embargo on all the participants in the war, including the internationally recognised Muslim-led Bosnian administration. Washington wanted to lift the embargo in the hope it would help Bosnian forces take on the Bosnian Serb army which had access to heavy weapons supplied by what was left of Yugoslavia. This comprised Serbia and Montenegro. The US also wanted to mount air strikes against Bosnian Serb military targets to help Bosnia fight back, which European governments fiercely opposed.'

'My Sophie you've certainly done your homework. But those political tensions occur during every conflict and Bosnia was no different.'

'Not according to Miss Aisha Abdallah. It was her opinion that it looked to the outside world as though an arms embargo was in place, but for UK forces to e able to hold key convoy routes, it became necessary to arm and fund factions of the community that would promise loyalty to the UK and US position; such was the importance of keeping those convoy routes open. That could not have been achieved in such terrain without the help of local people. Needless to say, some of those funds and military hardware found itself in the wrong hands. If this had come to the attention of the US, they may have begun a bombing campaign regardless of human cost.'

Peter was speechless and looked to Rebecca.

'Sophie darling, how can you possibly remember so much from school?'

'Don't be silly Mummy, I can't. I looked up my old project last night when I knew we were having this meeting. Do you want to see it?'

'No, I don't think that will be necessary. Would anyone like more coffee?'

'No thanks,' said Bob, 'we need to go and see Willie Dewar.' The meeting with Willie was arranged for the coming Monday afternoon but Bob had been thinking that if verisimilitude is good for one it may just be good for another.

#

Peter's description of the conflict was much the same as was playing out at Callum's that morning with Valerie. Despite her prodding, he explained how his role in Bosnia was basically that of a common soldier; his unit being intrinsically linked to the British efforts and overseen by the UN peacekeeping force. It was what he'd witnessed there that had caused him to get so upset the night before when he saw the painting.

Had Miss Abdallah, or indeed Sophie been on hand they might have asked more questions of Callum's role, but she wasn't and political history was not Val's strongpoint.

#

Bob returned to Rebecca's late afternoon. He and Sandra had spent the time walking down Cramond before she ran him to Portobello to collect his car. As he was leaving he asked whether she wished to join him for that hair of the dog but she declined on the auspices that she valued her friendship with Rebecca too much for such highjinks. That and the fact she thought it best to be sober, at least until her meeting with the cancer specialist the coming Monday morning.

#

He was pleased to see, as he pulled into the drive, that Rebecca's guests had gone and he began looking forward to an evening with her and Sophie He was also wondering if there would be any lamb left over from the previous night. As it turned out that was confirmed when he opened the front door and got the smell of lamb curry.

As he'd hoped, the evening passed with the three of them watching a movie that Sophie had chosen. The second it finished Bob stood and announced that an early night was in order.

If anyone who'd been at their meeting that morning had been asked what they thought Bob might dream about that night they might have answered Bosnia, or war, or espionage and the security services. But he hadn't. His dream involved Philip Gormand; a Philip Gormand less smartly dressed than when Bob had seen him on more than one occasion. This Philip Gormand was dripping wet and his clothes and skin were in shreds as he walked from the water of Windermere up the sand to the roadside.

CHAPTER THIRTEEN

Sunday 28th June

'Bobby, waken up!'

He could hear Rebecca's voice but it was as if something was dragging him back into sleep, into the dream.

'It's nearly ten o'clock.'

'Mummy, what's all the noise?'

'Sophie, Bob won't waken up, I'm really worried; maybe we should call the doctor.'

Just as she said this Bob moaned out loud and opened his eyes. 'What's, where…'

'You're with me Bobby, in my bed. You've been having a nightmare.'

'Sophie, I didn't know you were here,' stammered Bob, trying hard to sit upright.

'What were you dreaming of?' asked Rebecca.

'Dreaming doesn't describe it. It was our last case and the journey south with John Mackay. We were following Gormand. Even John was an ogre. I could swear it was real. That has never happened to me before.'

'Were you discussing Gormand with Sandra yesterday?'

'No. Wait a minute, yes. But it was Sean who mentioned him when he came in. That would be it. It must have triggered some sort of buried memory.'

'Or subconscious guilt being the more appropriate word.'

'What are you talking about woman?'

'John told me the day we went rallying. When you saw Gormand being ushered into the Russian car you said that the lakes were deep in Cumbria and Philip Gormand ended up being found drowned in one. Maybe on a subconscious level you're regretting not having stopped his killers when you had the chance. Just a thought?'

CHAPTER FOURTEEN

Monday 29th June

Bob had phoned Willie Dewar's house at nine and asked if it was okay to come at eleven instead of after noon. So, when he and Tracey arrived they expected Willie to be home but there was no answer at his door. Bob had been gracious enough to invite Rebecca too but she said she had an appointment with Mrs Spale to discuss future investments and such like, things he'd not understand.

'What's wie the gnomes?' asked Tracey as they waited for Willie to answer the door.

'Everyone that's crossed Willie Dewar's path gets the privilege of being remembered in the shape of one, without being asked of course.'

'That's weird, really weird.'

'Do you not think there's a lot of weird stuff going on with this case?'

'Aye.'

'Charles Molesworth's here. That's him over there in the centre, the one in the lawyer's wig.'

'That didn't take Mr Dewar long to make him. So, is everyone here dead?'

'They're gnomes Tracey, not real people.'

'But they represent real people don't they?'

'Aye, I suppose. Charles may have been here before he died. Play your cards right and you might end up here next.'

‘That gies me the creeps.’

Bob rang Willie’s doorbell one last time. ‘Maybe he’s round the back; he’s a keen gardener. You wait here.’ He disappeared around the side of the house and was away some minutes. When he reappeared, he was somewhat shaken and had his mobile phone to his ear. ‘Police and you’d better send an ambulance, though a hearse might be more apt.’

‘What is it?’

Willie Dewar, he’s dead.

‘What’s happened?’

‘No idea. I can’t see any signs of foul play, but then we couldn’t see any with Molesworth either.’

‘Are we gonnae run away this time?’

Bob didn’t answer but looked down at the gnome filled garden.

‘Maybe it’s another ghost?’

Completely ignoring her he turned and walked back around the house. Willie Dewar kept a neat garden and Bob was impressed. There was a greenhouse up the sloping garden full of tomato plants. On the left was a large hut, which Bob guessed might be the workshop where Willie manufactured his gnomes. But not anymore. The man was lying on his back almost under the potting bench that was fixed to the back wall of the pebble-dash house. There was a newly opened bag of compost on the bench with a half-filled terracotta pot beside it.

Bob was just about to check Willie’s pockets when a voice behind him stopped him in his tracks.

‘You can leave that to us now Mr James.’ It was Margaret Whalen.

He stood and turned. ‘I’m surprised to see you here Margaret, Willie Dewar’s hardly cauld yet; certainly not a job for the Cauld Case Squad.’

As Bob said this DI Sammy Brogue appeared. 'They're up to their eyes in it at Fettes and asked if we could take the call. It's that busy I'm surprised they've not asked you to make a comeback. Oh, I forgot, they have.'

'Now now Sammy, sarcasm doesn't become you.'

'Sorry Bob. Is this the bloke who made all those gnomes out front? I didn't see you there.'

'Not yet, not ever now by the look of things. We were due to interview Willie at eleven in relation to the Molesworth case.'

'I did see your secretary there right enough.'

'What?'

'In the flesh, not as a gnome.'

'How do you know she's my secr… No, don't bother to answer that. The canary birds must still be tweeting down your way.'

DI Brogue laughed out loud. 'So, what do you make of this?' He pointed to the body.

'Haven't a clue. No sign of violence. No bruising or wounds.'

'Natural causes?'

'Possibly.'

'Just like Charles Molesworth,' interrupted Margaret. 'You're still no further forward with that case. No wonder so many unsolved crimes end up on the CCS desk.'

'I think DC Whalen has spoken Sammy,' said Bob.

His slight didn't put her off. 'What are you doing here Bob? It's certainly not police business and more to do with your other interests.'

'Aye Willie, like myself, is a keen gardener, I should say was a keen gardener. I was here to pick his brains.' He turned to Sammy. 'Doing my own plot at the mo, Sam.'

'The plot thickens.'

Margaret tried again. 'Did they ever clear up that conflict of interest problem that you were continually accused of Bob?'

‘As a matter of fact they have. JP Associates are now working in conjunction with Police Scotland on the Molesworth case and that’s official. But then of course you weren’t at the meeting with MIT, were you Margaret?’

It was DI Brogue’s turn to interrupt proceedings. ‘It looks to me as if Willie Dewar has been dead for no more than a few hours at most. Mr Dewar was involved with Charles Molesworth in a court case against the Fishermens Union if memory serves me well. The death of Molesworth is an ongoing police enquiry.’

‘DI Sandra Laing asked me to help her look into the case and since she is feeling unwell she wants full reports from me. She’s been given the go-ahead from the Chief to involve our agency.’

Brogue spoke as he leaned over the body. If DI Laing is unwell she should not be receiving reports. I think it best if you leave this to us, don’t you?’

Bob couldn’t miss Margaret’s smile, nor her newly whitened teeth and was about to argue with the DI when Tracey touched him on the shoulder. She had her mobile phone in her hand. ‘That’s a call from Mark, he wants us to meet him at the office asap.’

Her boss looked in two minds whether to engage further with Brogue and Margaret or attend to the urgent call. He chose the latter and walked from the garden without a word. He didn’t speak until they were at the car. ‘What does he want?’

‘Who?’

‘Mark.’

‘Did A say that. A meant to say it was getting on past your brunch time, and A ken mair than most what you’re like on an empty stomach; those poor officers might have got the brunt of your hunger and have you bite their heads off.’

‘Aye, quite possibly. Thanks Tracey.’

‘I did phone Jo Molesworth while you were having your set-to with your ex-colleagues. We’re seeing her tomorrow at ten.’

#

‘A cannae believe this, ye’ve just had that hassle wie Margaret Whalen and her boss and now ye want tae take me intae Fettes canteen for brunch.’

‘They do a smashing fry-up and if we’ve played our cards right Bella will be behind the counter and we won’t need to eat for the rest of the day.’

What Bob excluded to mention about their visit to Police Scotland’s command centre was that he’d had enough remarks from officers about his “secretary” and wanted to see how they reacted when faced by the woman in person.

As it was, Bella was behind the counter. She looked as if she was well over seventy but Tracey could see that she obviously had a thing for Bob. It wasn’t the sexuality thing but more likely the son she’d never had and it showed in the amount of food she’d managed to cram onto his plate.

‘Bella, this is Tracey.’

‘Tracey? Not the secretary in the flesh. How are ye doing hen? Is this big bugger treating ye awright?’

‘Not bad Bella, but A could dae wie a rise.’

‘Well ye’ll wait a while. A’ve been waiting twenty years for a Christmas tip fae that yin.’

‘Now girls keep your voices down or you’ll be getting a man a bad name.’ He lifted his plate onto a tray and headed for the tables.

Tracey assumed he’d pick a quiet spot and was surprised to see him taking a seat at a large, busy table. When she joined him, she squeezed into the only space left.

‘Morning gents,’ said Bob, to no-one in particular. ‘This is my secretary and assistant investigator Tracey Cowan.’

For a second nobody spoke until one young constable lifted his plate. 'I'll see if I can find a quieter table.'

Two others went to do the same before Bob spoke. 'Was it something I said?'

He didn't get an answer.

'If you would just sit yourselves back down, this won't take a moment gentlemen. I think it would be in your best interest to hear what I've got to say.'

The three constables looked from one to the other then back to Bob. They sat down.

'It has come to our attention on more than one occasion recently that Tracey and JP Associates have become the subject of local gossip, both here and in Constitution Street nick, and I thought it best that you got the chance to meet us in person. We could answer any questions you may have concerning our set-up. So, if you want to fire away, we're all ears.'

Tracey couldn't believe her ears and waited for the result but not one word was forthcoming.

'I thought as much,' said Bob, as he buttered a roll. 'You obviously have nothing more to learn of our establishment so I will be very surprised if I hear another word about it.' He held the knife up. Do I make myself clear gentlemen?'

Tracey thought that one of the policemen was going to respond but then he appeared to have second thoughts.

'Bob looked directly at him. 'I know you son, you're the one that lost all his tyres outside North Telford Millennium Centre on Bonfire Night a year or two back.'

The lad's face turned red as his colleagues giggled quietly in the background.

'Now you can take yourselves off lads, to whichever hedge you crawled out from under, and let me get on with Bella's breakfast.'

As the table emptied a silence fell over Tracey and Bob until Bella appeared. 'Was it something you said? A've not seen that lot move as quickly, not even in an emergency.'

'One of them said he wasn't happy with the way you do your scrambled eggs so I had to have a word.'

'Which one?'

'Sorry Bella, that would be telling,' said Bob, handing over his plate. 'That was pure magic!'

She smiled broadly as she leaned over for Tracey's plate. 'What's wrong, are ye not hungry hen?'

'No Bella, A'm just not as hungry as A thought.'

'Yer not pregnant?' Bella put her hand to her own abdomen.'

'Heaven forbid. No, those days are well over.'

Bella's smile faded. 'A never had any.'

Tracey wanted to stand and give her a hug but after looking around the busy canteen thought better of it.

'Ma man was killed on the trawlers in Granton harbour when he was only nineteen. A winch cable broke.'

'A'm so sorry Bella.'

'I remember hearing about that,' said Bob. 'I was only about seven at the time but everybody spoke about it and about your man. They said he was a really nice lad.'

'Aye, that was ma Billy. A never married again.' She put the plates on her trolley and pushed it towards the kitchen.

'Billy Tait, that was it,' said Bob quietly.

Tracey sat in silence.

'Is everything alright?'

'Aye, it's just A wanted tae talk tae ye about something and now A've discovered your ma knight in shining tweeds A ken A've got the right man.'

'What is it? No, let me guess, it's Harry. Is he back at the nicking?'

‘No, it’s mair personal than that.’

‘What? Is it Tod?’

‘No. We shouldnae talk here? Could we maybe have a wee wander in Inverleith Park?’

‘Aye, come on, let’s get out of here.’

#

By the time they’d had their walk and got to Leith and the office, Bob had offered to have a word with Harry. Tracey only agreed if he promised not to put the frighteners on him as he had the constables back in Fettes.

But the case of Harry and Mrs Spale’s relationship would have to be put on hold. Standing outside the office was Dr Mark le Mot, and he wasn’t looking very happy.

CHAPTER FIFTEEN

Tuesday 30th June

Bob had a spring in his step as he and Tracey headed across the Links towards Jo Molesworth's.

'It must have been a good night boss,' said Tracey. 'A've not seen ye this animated in a long time. Has Rebecca come round to your charms again?'

'Not on your life. It's Mark.'

'Never thought you were his type.'

'Don't be facetious. It was something he told me in the Starbank. I knew he wasn't quite telling us everything yesterday and there was only going to be one way to get him to divulge the whole story.'

'Dinnae tell me, a bowl of olives?'

'Aye, and the rest. For a whippersnapper he can fairly put the grub away. After his aperitif, as he calls it, he had steak-pie and chips then had the cheek to ask to see the sweet menu.'

Tracey smiled to herself, remembering Bob's plateful at Fettes.

'Anyway, it was worth it. What he didn't tell us yesterday in here was that he believes Callum is quite unwell and not himself at all. He said they'd got on well in London and he was top of his game there and had managed to get promises of funding for their project. Mind you, according to Tod, promises of funding that come out of London don't always bear fruit.

'Poor Callum, has he got a bug?'

‘Aye, a bloody big one that could prove fatal.’ Bob sat down on a park bench. ‘Though Mark gave us a potted history of Callum’s time in Bosnia, it’s what Callum didn’t tell him that he believes is making him ill.’

‘What did he not tell him?’

‘What Callum’s role had been in that war.’

‘He was attached to Peter Blue’s contingent, wasn’t he?’

‘He was. What was asked of him and what he witnessed under Colonel Blue’s command was what caused him to retire from the forces and study for church ministry. If you read up on the UK involvement in Bosnia under the UN you will see a picture much as Callum told Mark and much as Peter had described at Rebecca’s. However what Daniel told Tod paints a whole different picture about Callum’s involvement.’

‘What was it?’

As the UK were bound up in peacekeeping duties and could not respond with force against the Serbians, much as the Americans wanted to do, the Brits began funding and arming militias to aid the task of keeping convoy routes open. The problem was that the militias way of doing things went way beyond any rules of conventional war. During his tour of duty Callum saw to the handover of finance and weaponry to the militias. He then witnessed many atrocities carried out by those militia groups. At one point he intervened and killed a militia leader. He was put on a charge by none other than Colonel Blue himself.

‘Goodness?’

‘Aye. If that information was ever allowed into the light of day it will certainly destroy Britain’s reputation for fairness and diplomacy.’

‘It will dae mair than that. Our special relationship wie America will be in tatters.’

‘Aye, that and our standing in the United Nations. That is what puts us all in danger, particularly Callum. I can see now why Daniel Manning was warning us off the Molesworth case.’ Bob stood. ‘Anyway, we’re about to find out from Jo if she discovered what her husband knew about Bosnia. Remember, she was his mental health nurse when he ended up in Andrew Duncan’s. He might have divulged things that should have remained hidden.’

#

Bob rang the bell and for some unknown reason did not think she would answer. It came as somewhat a surprise when she did, particularly when she ushered them in with a welcome more befitting close friends.

‘I’ve just filled the kettle.’ She pointed to the front room. ‘Help yourselves to a seat, won’t be a tick.’

Tracey was surprised too when she saw how old fashioned the room was, particularly when Jo’s dress sense was anything but conservative. The faded pink walls looked as if they’d been marbled and the black slate fireplace held ornaments one would expect to see in an old aunt’s house. A tiffany lamp with a dragonfly motif stood on a circular drawer chest beside the brass fender.

Bob chose an armchair by the fireplace while Tracey chose a chair at the dining table by the window.

‘I see you’ve made yourself comfortable. This is my favourite room. The house belonged to Charles’ aunt and she left it to him in her will. When we split he allowed me to live here. We were going to do it up and let it out, but there you go.’ Jo put the tray on the table. ‘I’ve not had time to do any modernisation yet.’

‘When exactly did you split?’ asked Bob.

‘There was no exact date. We just drifted apart gradually until we thought it best if we had places of our own. I’ve been here four years. That said, Charles and I remained friends and still saw each other on occasion. He wasn't the most stable of characters, especially after the war trials, and used to have nightmares and believe he was being haunted.'

'That's what we wanted to speak to you about,' said Bob.

'The nightmares?'

'No, the war trials. He ended up very ill and you were involved in his treatment and after care, is that right?'

'I wasn't the only one but yes I was designated Charles's main treatment nurse. But what has this got to do with his death?'

'It may have nothing to do with his death,' answered Tracey, but it helps if we can fill in all the gaps. Did you work with him for long?'

'It took all of a year to get him back on his feet enough to sign off treatment, but by then we had become an item, as they say, and it wasn't long after that we got married, much to the chagrin of his mother.'

'We've met his mother. She came to our office,' said Bob.

Jo turned to Tracey. 'Tracey, I can call you Tracey, can't I, knows all about Charles's problems in the Hague, don't you?'

'According tae what you told me when ye came tae the office.' answered Tracey. 'Charles's Mum painted a different picture of her son on her visit though.

'What point would there be in me lying about Charles's time in the Hague. He did meet a young Bosnian girl there and behaved in a way that was more than inappropriate. The fact that she was killed in an accident is probably what saved him from going on trial himself. You'll be able to check on the girl's existence and death in the Dutch press of the time.'

'Could your husband have learned anything from the girl that he divulged during his treatment,' asked Bob.

'I don't know what you mean.'

‘We believe she was in the Hague as a witness to atrocities in Bosnia and as Charles was one of many lawyers representing the victims, it makes sense that she would have shared her experiences with him.’

‘If she did I didn’t get to know about it. The only experiences that I got to know about were the ones she had with Charles in his hotel.’

‘So as far as you are aware the girl in question didn’t get a chance to testify before she was killed?’

‘As far as I know.’

‘You told Tracey that your husband liked the young girls of Leith too.’

‘Yes. He wasn’t as honest about that though but on more than one occasion I followed him. When I did challenge him about it he said it was none of my business. Looking back now it may be that Charles never found a cure for his illness and much of his behaviour towards me and the young girls could have stemmed from an unexpressed anger. We’ll never know that now though, will we?’

‘Who is your husband’s beneficiary?’ asked Tracey.’

‘I get everything: the houses, the business and all his savings and shares.’

‘That must account for a pretty penny,’ said Bob.

‘I wouldn’t know. That is all being taken care of by my solicitor.’ Jo walked over to the window that looked across the Links towards Charles’s house. ‘A room with a view. After we split up I used to stand here and look over to Queen Charlotte Street. I liked it there and strange though it may seem, I would much prefer that Charles was alive and we were still together.’

Aye right, thought Tracey as she stood to leave. Bob was thinking much the same as he took his cue from her.

#

‘Well that didn’t get us very far Dr Watson,’ said Bob as they walked up the garden path.

‘Far enough though.’

‘In what way?’

‘As far as Andrew Duncan’s. As she said herself, there was mair people treating Charles Molesworth than her. There would have been doctors, ward orderlies, and other mental health nurses. We just have tae find the right one.’

‘Good idea, for once. You’re becoming quite the sleuth are you not.’

‘Well someone’s got tae dae the thinking while you’re caught up in your relationship problems boss.’

‘Listen to who’s talking.’

‘Are we going back to the office?’

‘No, well you are, I’ve a visit to pay to someone I’ve not seen in a wee while.’

‘Not another woman?’

‘No, not this time.’

#

Having walked with Tracey back to Great Junction Street, Bob decided to take the number 22 bus to St. Andrew’s Square before walking the short distance to the offices of Spale Investment Company.

He didn’t wait long for the voice through the intercom. ‘Spale and Company, do you have an appointment?’

How friendly he thought. ‘It’s the police.’

‘Just a moment.’ The lock opened and Bob pushed hard at the large Georgian door.

‘I’m here to see Mrs Spale.’ As he said this to the receptionist, Harry Cowan’s head popped up from under the counter.

‘Bob, what are you daen here?’

‘Never mind me. What are you doing there?’

‘Rerunning some cables for the new computers.’

‘I was hoping to see Evelyn Spale, but you’ll do. Is there somewhere we can talk?’

‘Sounds serious.’

‘It is.’

‘Follow me, we can go tae ma office.’

Bob followed Harry down a steep spiral staircase to the basement and a door that read **CONCIERGE**.

‘This is ma new office. When Gormand was here I had the broom cupboard.’ Harry spoke as he unlocked the door.

‘I heard you’d come up in the world.’ He followed Harry into the room and closed the door behind him.

‘What dae ye mean?’

‘You and Mrs Spale.’

‘What’s Tracey been saying?’

‘That you and your boss are spending too much time together. She’s worried Harry.’

‘Oh Bob, she’s nothing tae worry about. A dinnae ken how she got this intae her daft heid.’

‘I think it has something to do with the fact you hardly ever come home before seven and your spending more and more time with your boss.’

‘Aye, but it’s not what she thinks.’

‘Listen Harry, Tracey’s not as daft as you think and if I were you I’d pay heed to that, or you might end up out on your ear and I don’t think Evelyn Spale is worth that, do you?’

Harry was about to argue when the door opened and Evelyn entered. ‘Hello Bob, I thought it might be you, particularly when Mary announced that a very handsome policeman had disappeared with Harry to his office. What brings you to our neck of the woods?’

'Mrs Spa…Evelyn, did Mary leave out the word "elderly"? I was just passing and thought I'd pop in. From the guarded welcome I received through your intercom I thought it best to use my old designation.'

'You merely passing? On your way to your club perhaps?' She was referring to the Masonic Lodge directly across from her office.

'As a matter of fact I am.'

'Well don't let us keep you. Harry, are you remembering we have a meeting at five-thirty tonight?'

'Aye, Evel…Mrs Spale.'

#

Evelyn said she'd see Bob out but when they reached the top of the spiral stair and he turned towards the front door she put her finger to her lips and beckoned him to follow her. She opened the last door in the corridor and ushered him into the broom cupboard.

'Harry's old office?'

'He told you.'

'Yep.'

What else did he tell you?'

'That his wife Tracey has absolutely no need to be concerned about his coming home late from work most nights and his spending more and more time with his boss.'

Evelyn laughed. 'I thought that might be why you're here; you think Harry's my toy boy.'

'What's so funny about that?'

'Nothing, except that it couldn't be further from the truth.'

'That's what they all say.'

'Bob, I would have preferred not to have to tell you what I am about to tell you, but I respect you, and I like Tracey very much. I certainly don't want her getting the wrong end of the stick. Nor do I want anything to happen to her marriage.'

CHAPTER SIXTEEN

Wednesday 1st July

'Ye could have phoned me last night! I nearly threw him out. I had his bags packed for him when he got hame.'

'Aye, sorry about that. I didn't want to tell you over the phone. Eveyln took me into the broom cupboard to tell me, it's that secret.'

'You could have come tae the house.'

'No, I've enough war zones to be getting on with at present without dealing with yours and Harry's'

'Very funny.'

Tracey and Bob were in the office and he'd just told her the real reason for Harry's late homecomings.

'Let me get this right. Your telling me that the two Russian oligarchs who remained in Gormand's tontine are putting pressure on Spale Investment Company tae come up with the remaining funds and that Harry and Mrs Spale are going after them and Harry has got Hacker Hanson involved?'

'That's exactly what I'm telling you. They're trying to put together a case against them before going to the FSA and the police.'

'A knew ma Harry was glaikit, but A didnae realise how glaikit. Does he no ken that some oligarchs kill people?'

'That's why I couldn't phone you last night. The three musketeers might have the knowledge and skills to keep the

Russians in the dark about their research but it would only take one slip-up and they could all end up sleeping with the fishes.'

'Aye, like Gormand. A've heard many a reason why a wife shouldnae chastise her man for gaun out wie another woman but this takes the biscuit.'

'That's what I thought. On the subject of biscuits, do we have any?'

'What, did darling Beccy not give you breakfast this morning?'

'I stayed at my own place.'

'You'd better watch out or it will be your stuff in a bag waiting for you when you get back to Cramond.'

'Aye maybe.' He went to the kitchen.

'The biscuits, the fresh ones, are in the tin on the top shelf. And mind A take two sugars in ma coffee.'

He reappeared with two steaming mugs and a plate of figs rolls and took a seat at the coffee table. 'Did you manage to get hold of anyone at Andrew Duncan's?'

'Aye.'

'Well are you not going to share it with me?'

'We've an appointment there at eleven so we'd better get a move on.'

He nearly spat his coffee over the table.

#

'This must be the worst town in Europe to drive in,' It had taken them all of forty-five minutes to get to Morningside from Leith and Bob wasn't happy. 'We're going to be late.'

Tracey pointed at the passing buildings. Isn't that where Jan Keen's teacher lives?'

'Agnes. Can't quite remember her last name. She was lovely, but a right nervous soul. She had fig rolls in her biscuit barrel too.'

'Ye cannae remember her name but ye can remember what biscuits she had in the house.'

'It will come to me. Who is it we are seeing at the clinic?'

'A told ye that in the office. Is your memory awright? Doctor Paul Rose. He was a young houseman when Molesworth was here and the receptionist thinks he sat in on one or two of Molesworth's treatments. I asked about records, but all paper records were destroyed about three years ago.'

'Nobody's bought me a crossword puzzle book yet, if that's what you mean?'

'What's that got to do wie anything?'

'A couple of pals of mine took dementia and the first thing their families did, prior to official diagnosis mind you, was buy them a puzzle book to keep their brain active. So this Dr Rose still works here?'

'Obviously, but he's a consultant now and his time is precious, or so A was told.'

They were shown to the waiting room by the same woman who'd answered the phone to Tracey. When she turned her back on them they both agreed, in lowered voices, that the description "frosty-faced" seemed apt.

After a twenty-minute wait, Bob was about to enquire with the receptionist as to the hold-up when a man in his mid-forties appeared.

'Tracey, is it?'

'Aye…yes.'

'And this will be the one you said would be arriving with you?'

Bob stood quickly and put out his hand. 'Bob James.'

The speed of Bob's movements took the psychiatrist by surprise, causing him to step back slightly. He shook Bob's hand with an outstretched arm. 'You'd better come to my office.'

After walking a very long corridor they came to a door marked **Dr P. Rose Psychiatrist.** 'They put my name on the door. I sometimes wonder if that's in case I forget where I'm going.'

That's better, thought Bob.

Dr Rose directed them to the two chairs opposite him across his desk. The investigators waited for him to remove his notebook from his satchel. 'My receptionist said you were interested in the case of a Charles Molesworth dating back to the mid-nineties.'

'That's correct,' answered Bob.

He put the notebook on the desk and opened it. 'You'll have to bear with me, these are the only notes I have from the time. All other records would have been destroyed when we updated our systems.'

If Tod were here, thought Bob, he'd be thinking conspiracy. 'You were a houseman at the time?'

'Yes that's correct. My superior, Professor Granger, passed away recently. He would have been able to help you better than I.'

'What can you tell us of that time?' asked Tracey.

'It's only a few scribbles really and only two pages worth. They're mostly academic short notes and very messy. Charles was in a bad way when he came in and one of the worst cases we'd seen of PTSD.'

'PTSD?' asked Tracey.

'Post-Traumatic Stress Disorder. The extent of Charles's condition was more akin to that of soldiers from the front line. But he was a lawyer and his PTSD was a consequence of the war crimes trials in The Hague. Very interesting case and very unusual. If I remember correctly it was the death of his lead witness, a young Bosnian Girl, Anna was the name he kept repeating. She was killed when a truck left the road and hit her as she stood on the pavement waiting for Charles. He saw the whole thing, poor man.'

'How do you know all that?'

‘Because Charles kept repeating her name over and over and in time Professor Granger was able to get him to relive the whole event.’

‘And what did your Professor think of all this?’ asked Bob.

‘He was obviously very concerned for the patient and at one point put him on twenty-four-hour surveillance, or suicide watch in ordinary parlance.’

It was Tracey’s turn again. ‘Do you think this was a genuine case of PTSD. I have heard of people faking the condition to enable them to escape from responsibility or prevent them from playing their part in any future conflict.

‘Have you reason to believe that Charles was doing that?’

It was Bob’s turn again. ‘What about Professor Granger, would he have kept any private notes at home?’

‘Possibly, but if he had they’d no longer exist.’

‘Why is that?’

‘Oh, didn’t I say? He died in a house fire. His villa in the Grange was completely destroyed.’

Bob turned to look at Tracey. ‘I think it’s time we were going, don’t you? Dr Rose doesn’t seem to be in a position to be able to help us in finding Charles’s killer.’

The Professor’s swivel chair shot back as if it had been pushed by some invisible force. ‘Charles is dead?’

‘You’ll need to watch for the whiplash with that chair Dr Rose. That is why we are here. He was murdered.’ Bob stood. ‘If you don’t mind my asking Professor, you’ve been using the deceased’s first name continually throughout this interview, is that normal practice?’

He took a moment to answer. ‘No, sorry, it’s not common practice.’

‘Why use it then?’

He thought for a moment. 'I met him a time or two after he left us. Professor Granger was interested in following up on the case and he and Charles eventually became friends. I was invited, on more than one occasion, to dinner with them at the Professor's house.'

'Is that allowed?' asked Tracey.

'Strictly speaking it is not encouraged, but there was no harm in it. In fact it may have been the catalyst in helping Charles find a cure.'

'But there was another catalyst wasn't there Paul.' Bob put his hands on the desk.

'I don't know what you mean.'

'We think you do. What about Jo Molesworth, she befriended him, didn't she?'

'Oh, Jo, of course. You know about her?'

'Know what about her?'

'When Charl…Mr Molesworth was here, Jo was one of his mental health nurses. Unfortunately, she had to be removed from his case.'

'Why,' asked Tracey.

'She wouldn't leave him alone. It was becoming very embarrassing for the other staff and Professor Granger decided it best for all concerned if she be removed. But that didn't stop her and she was in his room at every opportunity. Eventually the Professor had her reassigned to work with patients in recovery at the Astley Ainslie Hospital. He even took the step of informing Security that on no account was she to be allowed in here. But as you probably know, once Charles was released from our care it didn't take her long to find him.'

'She married him. Did you know that?'

'Yes. Truth is I suspected that was why Professor Granger befriended him. I think he felt somewhat responsible for that, and I'm not sure he thought she was good for Charles.'

Bob stood. 'Thank you Dr Rose, you have been very helpful.'

The doctor stood and leaned over the desk to shake their hands. 'Do you wish me to see you out?'

'No, that won't be necessary,' answered Bob.

'I'm not quite sure what your vocation was Mr James but I believe you'd have made a super psychiatrist.'

#

As the two sleuths were making their way from the hospital to Bob's car, Tracey pulled at his arm. 'What about Mrs Spale, Harry and the Oligarchs, Dr Freud?'

'I think we've done enough for one day, don't you? I'll need to get my head around all this.'

It may well have been the case that they'd done enough for one day, had it not been a Wednesday. Tracey would be working with Tod Peterson that night in Edinburgh Prison.

CHAPTER SEVENTEEN

Thursday 2nd July

'Why did you not answer your phone last night?' Bob was in the office very early and Tracey and Bertie had just come in. The dog wagged his tail when Bob spoke.

'A was working and had my mobile off. A saw that you'd phoned when Harry was picking me up after the class.'

'I forgot that you'd be working with Tod last night. If I'd remembered I'd have warned you not to mention Mrs Spale's situation to him. That's why I was trying to get you, before you saw him.'

'It's Harry's situation too.'

'Aye, but it's Mrs Spale's business.'

'What about me? It's my business when ma man is in danger.'

'Oh, he's your man now? I thought you were throwing him out. Did you tell Tod that Harry was in danger?'

'What dae you think?'

He stood up from behind the computer. 'That wasn't a good idea Tracey.'

'Remind me why not?'

'You know as well as I do. Tod has friends in high, dark places and we don't want him getting into any more trouble than he's already in. Remember he'll be sent to an open prison within the year and released not long after, if he plays his cards right. But if he gets himself involved in this business with the tontine he might never see the light of day.

‘Neither will we, but we’ve got tae dae something tae help Mrs Spale and Harry.’

‘So, what did you tell Tod?’

‘A didnae have tae tell him, he already knew.’

‘Apparently you talk in your sleep and Rebecca thought it prudent tae phone Tod and tell him all you said.’

‘I do not talk in my sleep!’

‘How dae ye ken, if ye’re sleeping?’

‘What really happened Tracey?’

‘Rebecca got a call fae Evelyn Spale. She told your beloved everything about the tontine, including that you’d been tae the office in George Street. After her call Rebecca phoned Tod. She’s no daft that one eh.’

‘And she told Tod everything?’

‘And more.’

‘What?’

‘That she’s worried about your relationship. That you’re spending mair and mair time in Portobello wie Sandra.’

‘She told him that?’

‘She loves you Bob James and the quicker you get that through your thick skull the better.’

‘We’re all going to need thick skulls after what you and Rebecca have told Tod. Now we are up to our eyes in international politics, espionage and money laundering.

‘Well if JP Associates is that busy wid ye mind getting out fae behind ma desk and let me get tae work. A think a diagram of events might be not a bad idea. The way things are stacking up, we’re gonnae need one.’

CHAPTER EIGHTEEN

Friday 3rd July

Bob and Rebecca were seeing Sophie onto the bus at Cramond Village, before they headed to Leith and the office. Sophie was going into town to meet Mark; Bob had offered her a lift, which was politely refused.

They watched as she took her seat at the rear of the bus and half expected her to turn round and wave but she didn't bother to look back.

'Would you credit that,' said Rebecca, 'I've not been able to get her out of the house since that awful time in Cambridge and one phone call from Dr Mark le Mot inviting her to meet him for coffee and she is out of the door without a by your leave.'

'That was a terrible time for her. She's done well surviving, never mind getting out of the house. She's a great lass your Sophie. You'll miss her when she starts university again.'

'Yes, but at least it's not Cambridge. She'll be staying at home, thank goodness. Sophie has been through so much in her short life and seen things that no girl her age should have seen.'

'Aye.'

'You were the first person she confided in. I do wonder sometimes exactly why she chose you?'

'Perhaps because I'd been a policeman?'

'No, it was more than that. I think she saw you as a potential replacement to that horror she was forced to call father. And you didn't divulge her secret, not even to me. Was that because you thought I already knew?'

'No. Sophie asked me to tell no-one, not even you.'

I think she's adopted you, you know.'

'Aye.'

'Why don't you bite the bullet and become the father she so needs.'

'Is this a proposal Rebecca Stark?'

'I hadn't thought of that.'

'Yes.'

'Pardon?'

'Aye, I accept. Now are you going to get down on one knee?'

By the time they arrived at the office, Tracey was already there and had her diagram on the smartboard. She also had a plate of doughnuts and three mugs on the coffee table. 'You two look awfie happy, is there something A should know?'

Bertie looked up from his basket and shook his floppy ears.

'No, we're just taken aback by your diagram,' answered Bob. 'It's fairly cheered us up, that and the doughnuts of course.'

'Well if you're that cheery one of you could put the kettle on while I'm getting the presentation ready.'

'I'll get it,' answered Rebecca, bouncing like a schoolgirl into the kitchen.

'Well?' asked Tracey, under her breath.

'We're getting married.'

Bertie got up and wagged his tail.

Tracey was obviously taken aback but in her normal fashion tried to hide it. 'It's about bloody time.'

'I agree. She proposed this morning.'

'She proposed! She did not!'

'She did, and she's going to ask you to be her bride's maid. She said you'll need to go for elocution lessons first though.'

'What?'

'Only joking, but she is going to ask you.'

'What about your best man?'

'Aye, that's a problem, unless they let him out for the day.'

'Either that or you could get married in the clink.'

'I'm sure Beccy would…' Bob said no more as his fiancée returned from the kitchen with a cafetière of coffee. 'Are you ready with your presentation Tracey?'

'Nearly. That was quick Beccy, Bob and I were just catching up.'

Must be learning the tools of benevolent lying in her sojourns to the prison thought Bob.

'Right. This presentation is in part thanks tae Harry. He came here last night straight from work and we finished it together. We didnae get hame till after eleven.'

Bob couldn't help smile at her use of "we" in referring to her and Harry. A few days ago, she was for throwing him into the street.

'We'll make sure that you are recompensed for that, and Harry too.'

Bob's smile faded. 'Well can we get on with the diagram before we start dishing out the overtime.'

Tracey called up the first slide.

Slide 1. Monday 8th June:

Charles Molesworth approaches JP Associates and says he is being haunted in his home. His home in Queen Charlotte Street doubles as his office.

Bob coughed somewhat too loudly.

Slide 2. Tuesday 9th June:

Bob James and Tracey Cowan attend client's home at his request. They find him dead. After a brief search of the premises they abandon the property and telephone the police, anonymously.

‘Bobby explained the situation to me when he got home,’ added Rebecca. ‘I didn’t particularly think that was such a good idea leaving the scene. Interestingly sometime later Sandra phoned Bob to tell him she’d been given the Molesworth case.’

‘Aye alright. She actually phoned to tell me my central heating boiler wasn’t working. Now can we just get on with it.’

Tracey ignored the outburst. ‘Perhaps you could fill us in on what happened when you went with Sandra to Molesworth’s house?’

He took some moments before answering. ‘When we got into the house Sandra called from the first-floor landing; there was something she wanted me to see. When I reached the landing, I expected to see her in the bedroom where Molesworth was found dead but instead she was standing by a narrow doorway to the left of the deceased room and beckoned me to follow her. When I got to the doorway in question I was surprised to see her climb a narrow spiral staircase. “This leads to the attic,” she called back. I had to stoop to avoid the low ceiling as I followed her up. She then opened another narrow door, causing cobwebs and dust to float downwards all over me. When I got to the attic I was busy dusting myself down then realised Sandra was staring at the floor. When I followed her gaze I could hardly believe what I was seeing. There was an occult pentagram drawn on the floor in the centre of the room. Naturally we assumed that our Mr Molesworth was into black magic or some sort of devil worship. No wonder he thought he was being haunted, he’d old Nick living in the attic.’

‘Thank you for that Bob. A think we can move on fae here now though,’ said Tracey, calling up the next slide.

Slide 3. Monday 15th June

BJ and TC visit Fishermens Union and meet with Willie Dewar. Other than the story of Brian Scott, the ex-trawlerman who fell into the docks while delivering a letter for the Union, Mr Dewar didn't have much to say about Molesworth. The lawyer had won two and a half million pounds for his client on the grounds that Brian Bain should never been sent into the docks when the Union had firm knowledge of his alcohol problem. Unfortunately, Molesworth client was never able to enjoy the fruits of his win and is now in a very expensive care-home in Ravelston suffering from alcoholic dementia.

Tracey looked at Bob as she said those last words.

'What are you looking at me for?' asked Bob. As an aside, Callum Mackie believes there was a case to answer.'

'If I may continue?'

'This alcoholic dementia made it impossible for Brian to be interviewed. It appears that the only winner in this whole sad affair was Molesworth through his exorbitant fees.'

'And that's where his wife, Jo Molesworth, comes in. She's certainly a winner now that her husband is dead,' added Bob.

'And that's why Willie Dewar was a suspect, the fact that Molesworth nearly bankrupted the Union?' asked Rebecca.

'He wasn't actually a suspect,' answered Bob, 'but was under investigation. That was until his death of course. There is no way on God's earth we will find out anymore regarding the Fishermens Union now that Willie is dead and Brian Bain is suffering from dementia.'

'Does that not tell you something?' Rebecca poured herself another coffee but still resisted the doughnuts.

'What?' asked Bob, looking at the empty cafetière.

'Mr Dewar could have been killed to cover up his involvement. If he was involved and paid someone to do Molesworth a harm then that someone is maybe covering his own tracks.'

'Why would Willie want to do that?'

'To keep the good name of the Union intact perhaps? Or sheer revenge?'

'I agree,' added Tracey.

'You two are worse than that bunch of dunderheads at Fettes. Anyway, we'll have to await the autopsy on Willie. In the meantime, I'll away and fill that empty coffee pot.'

As he walked to the kitchen Tracey and Rebecca smiled to each other. 'Maybe we should wait for his return before we continue?' said Rebecca.

'Aye.'

'Just as well,' said Bob as he returned from the kitchen with a full cafetière. 'These walls have ears.'

'Then there is Jo Molesworth, a very strange kettle of fish,' said Tracey.

'Talking about kettles of fish,' said Bob, 'when Sandra and I returned to Molesworth's for a second visit, I had Bertie with me and he wouldn't go into the deceased's bedroom. Turns out pepper spray had been used in the room and it scares the hell out of dogs. What do you think that was about?'

'Surely it was to scare Molesworth's dog.' said Rebecca.

'If that's the case, then the implication is that there was an intruder in the house that night and he needed that dog subdued.'

'And he kent that Molesworth had a dog. Or he widnae have taken the spray wie him. Whoever it was knew the lawyer.'

'He, or she,' said Bob. 'Anyway, what if Molesworth himself had used the spray. I've seen it used to ward off the most evil of characters. Maybe he thought it could do the same with devils?'

Both women ignored Bob's point.

'That brings us back tae Jo Molesworth,' said Tracey with a look of disdain. 'She has the most tae gain fae her man's death and she is one hard nut tae crack. She's obviously spinning us a line about the young Bosnian girl Anna. Jo wants us to believe that her husband was abusing his position and having sex with a minor.' Tracey remembered about Sophie's abuse the second she'd said this and began fumbling her words.

'It's okay Tracey,' said Rebecca.

'How do you know he wasn't? asked Bob. He could have been, we cannot know for certain that his tirades whilst in hospital weren't because of his guilt. We are never going to know that for sure.'

'Never say never, darling. I might have an idea that may allow us to get closer to the real Jo Molesworth.' Rebecca lifted a doughnut, studied it then replaced it.

'What idea might that be?' Bob lifted the doughnut she'd just put down and took a large bite.

'She is the sole heir to his estate, which of course includes the Georgian house and office, her own house and the continued income from her husband's company should she choose to continue. As you know, property and investment is something that I have learned much about in the last few years and I have a large property portfolio run under the name of Stark Estates, Property Management Company. Mrs Molesworth has never met me but that could easily be arranged simply by putting a letter through the door in Queen Charlotte Street with an offer to purchase the property for letting purposes. That may enable us to ascertain whether she is indeed in this for the money.'

'Brilliant,' answered Tracey.

'If she does have her eye on the prize, I could exploit her weakness. I could indicate how much can be made from property speculation, subtly of course, and maybe even offer her involvement in my business. After all, the property game can be ever so rewarding but awfully lonely for a woman on her own.'

'Am I hearing right?' asked Bob putting down his mug too hard.

'Aye,' said Tracey. 'What a great idea eh?'

'I think I'll take Bertie for a walk.'

Bertie jumped out of his basket wagging his tail and ran over to him. 'You'd better get your lead Bertie, we're going to be away a while.'

CHAPTER NINETEEN

Wednesday 8th July

'Have you seen the man sitting directly outside of our office Harry?'

'No. What man?'

'He appeared about an hour ago. I saw a passerby from the window. She was bending down and had a five-pound note in her hand. I went out to see what she was doing and she had put the note into the hat of an old beggar. He is sitting with his back to our office wall.'

'A'll go and have a look,' said Harry, moving at lightning speed toward the door.

When he returned he looked somewhat dazed.

'Is he still there?'

'Aye he is Mrs Spale.'

'Did you ask him if he wouldn't mind moving on?'

Harry thought for a second. 'A did, but he just ignored me.'

'Shouldn't you try again?'

'He's a big bloke.'

'Maybe he'll move on of his own volition soon enough. Perhaps we'll leave it for now.'

Good idea thought Harry, his mind jumping back to the night in Murrayfield when that same man all but saved his life. If he's chosen to sit out there now it's for a reason and more than likely that reason is for our protection.

#

It had taken until Tuesday 7th for Jo Molesworth to contact Rebecca. Their meeting was then arranged for the Wednesday at eleven. Rebecca had insisted they meet near to the property in question and chose Malmaison on the Shore. Always good for impressing the wary seller, she thought when she hung up.

Tracey had described Jo as Hippy like with a disheveled manner but that is not what walked into the hotel bar. The grieving widow was in a black suit and had her hair tied much as Rebecca's in a French bun. The only sign of the danger Bob banged on about when he returned with Bertie, was the bright red velvet scarf tied tightly at her neck. Bob James does go worrying himself over much she was thinking as she stood to welcome her guest. 'Mrs Molesworth, Rebecca Stark. Do you wish coffee?' They shook hands.

'Fruit tea if they have it. Chamomile and ginger preferably.'

'Thank you for agreeing to meet with me.'

'I was intrigued when I read your letter, though I've no intention of selling. Charles has only been dead little more than a month.'

'Yes, and it can take months and sometimes years to wind up an estate.'

'That's not what I meant.' Jo went quiet for a moment. 'Were you aware that my husband had died when you had the letter put through our door?'

'No, I am sorry. I didn't know.'

'Then how could you know that the property may go on the market, or indeed who I was?'

Rebecca was completely unprepared for Jo's questioning. 'I, we have ways of property searching that keeps us ahead of the game. My researcher never divulges where he gets his information of course. It helps keep him in a job.'

‘No, but your researcher obviously has ways that let you know when someone’s property might end up on the market, and nine times out of ten that must be because the person has died?’

‘Well, yes, but it’s not quite as cut-throat as it sounds. Some partners of the deceased may want or need the profit from property to support their lifestyle.

Jo thought for a moment. ‘And you believe I might be one of those?’

‘Not at all, but it does happen, believe me.’

‘What is it you want from me Mrs Stark? Whatever it is, perhaps some honesty would be a good starting point?’

‘Yes of course. You’re correct in what you say. Our company, like many others, employs freelance searchers who continually scour the market for potential properties and flag them up. I’m sorry if we’ve jumped the gun here. We can forget the whole thing.’

‘Who is the “we” in your company?’

Rebecca looked distinctly uncomfortable and turned around to look for table service before turning back to face her interrogator. ‘Actually, there is no “we”, I am sole proprietor of the company.’

‘Oh, I see. I couldn’t help notice your business address is Gamekeepers Road.’

‘Yes I work from home.’

‘Much as my husband did before his death. Were you married to Richard Stark the banker?’ She left out “and paedophile”.

‘You know about that?’

‘I think all of Edinburgh and most of Scotland knows about it Mrs Stark.’

‘Yes, well…Call me Rebecca, please.’

‘During my mental health nursing studies, I had one or two lectures from Dr Keen; when I saw her name in relation to your husband’s case I couldn’t help but follow proceedings.’

Rebecca's face reddened and she wondered what else Jo Molesworth knew about her, including the JP Associates connection. 'My business and property portfolio has nothing to do with Richard, or Dr Keen, if that makes you feel more comfortable. I inherited a large legacy which included some properties, from my uncle and being on my own and wishing to take the dreadful occurrences off my mind I registered as a company.'

'Where is your daughter now?'

'She starts university in October, Edinburgh.'

'What is she studying, if you don't mind me asking?'

'Psychology.'

'How interesting. I did a degree in psychology and chose mental health nursing as my career choice.'

'Are you still working?'

'No, I gave up years ago. Why do you ask?'

'Oh, it's nothing. Well I was just thinking maybe you could help Sophie with her studies, just to get her off on the right footing?'

'For a moment there I thought you were going to offer me a job.' For the first time since her arrival, Jo laughed.

'What would you say if I did? Someone with your skills and background in psychology might be just what's needed. It can be very lonely having to make all the decision on one's own.'

'I'd say, forget the fruit tea. They stock a rather lovely Leith Claret here.'

By mid-afternoon Jo had explained everything about her husband, how she met him and his penchant for young girls which led to his downfall.

Rebecca, on the other hand, spent the hours describing in detail the value of her assets and how much she was looking forward to being able to share her future with such a like-minded person as Jo Molesworth.

#

By three o'clock Tracey was well and truly fed up. She'd been watching Bob pace the office floor since lunchtime and could take no more. 'A'm going out!'

'Where are you off to?'

'Anywhere that gets me out of here. A've been watching you go back and forwards between ma desk and the front door for two hours and A cannae take any mair.'

'No bloody wonder! She was meeting Jo Molesworth at eleven o'clock and it's gone three and there's still no sign of her!'

'Rebecca's a big girl. Why don't you take your mind off it and cut her some slack? You can come wie me.'

'That's maybe not a bad idea, but only if you cut out the clichés.' He went to the coat stand and lifted his jacket. 'Right.'

As they turned into Henderson Street they walked straight into Harry. 'What are you daen here at this time?' asked Tracey. 'Should you not be getting ready tae go wie Mrs Spale for after work drinkies?'

'I could do with one of those myself,' answered Bob.

'Dinnae go on about that again Tracey. A found something out at work that A think ye should know about. Trouble is the way things are now, A cannae phone or email so Evelyn said it was okay tae come tae see ye in person.'

'What is it?'

'Can we go back tae the office? It's important.'

'No, A'm not going back in there, not for aw the tea in China. What is it?'

Harry looked around to see that no-one was listening. 'Hacker's been helping us wie the oligarchs, and A told him about Molesworth. He's been able tae get a fix on Jo Molesworth's phone. You told me she had her door cam rigged up tae it so A asked him if there was anywie he could access the cam. It took him aw of half an hour.'

'That's great news, what did he find out?' asked Bob.

'That she's been getting a regular visitor.' Harry took out his phone and called up the video and turned the screen to face Bob.

'Chri…I'd swear that's the bloke who was driving the black van at Leith Links just after we started on the case.'

'Well whoever he is,' said Harry, 'he's never away fae the place.' He put his phone back into his pocket. 'Listen, A've got tae go, A've tae help Evelyn lock up.' He winked at Tracey as he turned away then turned back. 'Oh aye, there's one other thing, Daniel Manning is sitting begging outside Spale and Co.' Then he was off like a bat out of Hell.

'What now?' asked Bob. 'We should really go to Spale and Co and ask Daniel what he is up to.'

'A disagree. Why don't we pay a visit tae Callum? A think he's got some questions tae answer that might help us get closer tae our Jo Molesworth, if Rebecca hasnae already done so. Evelyn can wait.'

#

It took them fifteen minutes to walk to the Water of Leith and cross over the river to Callum's office. The large iron studded door was locked. They pressed the intercom. 'Yes?' It was Mark.

'JP Associates.'

'Yes? Do you have an appointment?'

'I'll appointment you! Are we getting in or do we have to knock the door down?'

'You'd need a battering ram to do that.' They could almost see Mark smile behind the heavy oak and only had to wait a few seconds before the door creaked open and they could see his smile for real. 'Welcome to Beyond.' He stepped aside to beckon them in.

‘We expected Lurch to open that door,’ said Bob.

‘Not our choice of door exactly. It’s a replica of the original fifteenth century one. This used to be a church.’ The building has class A conservation so we can do nothing about it.’

‘It was the original St. Ninians Kirk,’ answered Tracey. ‘Then it went on to become North Leith Parish Church.’

‘Someone mentioned that. There’s some very interesting symbols in the plaster work from that period.’

‘Is Callum available?’ asked Bob, with more than a hint of impatience.

Mark looked to Tracey for a sign of why Bob was so abrupt. ‘He’s busy at the moment but shouldn’t be much longer.’

‘A client?’

‘No. We have involved a local pharmacist in BEYOND. She is bringing us up to speed about recreational drugs and prescribed medications.’

‘Methadone?’ asked Tracey.

‘That’s one of them,’ replied Mark, just as Callum’s office door opened and Daniella came out. She swerved passed the three associates and disappeared.

Callum leaned on the door frame and looked out to see that she had gone. When he closed the door and turned they could see that his face was tinged red. ‘Bob, a sight for sore eyes indeed. I heard your voices and was able to tell Ms Mobuto that I’d forgotten I had an appointment. Thanks for that.’

‘Some difficulties?’ asked Bob.

‘I’ve just spent the last hour trying to explain how the name “Beyond” describes our project.’ He looked at Mark, who looked down at the floor.

‘Ye could always change the name,’ said Tracey.

‘Too late for that. All the admin is in place, including funding applications, letterheading etcetera, etcetera.’

‘Oh well,’ answered Bob, ‘that’s that then.’

‘Come away in and we’ll get the kettle on. Mark, would you mind nipping round the corner for some buns?’

For a second Dr Le Mot thought Callum was going to ask him to get whisky and was about to object then turned without a word and left.

‘A’ll chum Mark,’ said Tracey, following him.

‘Take a pew, as they say in the best establishments. Is this merely a social call or are you in need of some spiritual intervention?’

‘No, it’s no social call but before I end up on prescribed drugs I need some information regarding your involvement in the Bosnian War and in particular if you have had any dealings with Charles Molesworth lawyer.

‘You are getting very serious in your old age Bob. Tracey and I have spoken at length about your case with particular reference to whether his death could have been caused by evil spirits. But my only real knowledge of Charles Molesworth is having come across his name in my studies of Leith shipping, and as pastor to seamen. I learned about the case against the Fishermens Union and in a strange way I agreed with Molesworth. That chap should never have been sent into the docks with the letter. His fall was an accident waiting to happen.’

‘Is that your only knowledge of the lawyer?

‘I’m afraid so.’

‘What about the war trials in the Hague? And why did you react so badly to the painting in Valerie’s house?’

‘So that was a set-up; I might have guessed that JP Associates was behind that little show. It does surprise me that Valerie went along with it though.’ He thought for a moment. ‘If you must know, what happened in Bosnia really upset me, and still does. The Falklands was one thing and bad things happened there, but the Balkans was quite another; People were neighbours one day and killing each other the next. Atrocities everywhere. You've not been in a war zone, have you Bob?'

'Aye, alright. So you know nothing about the trials?'

'No. After the war in Bosnia I gave up the military and began studying for the ministry. It was that war that helped me make my decision.'

'So why are you still at Peter Blue's beck and call?'

'You've certainly got your sources. The Security Services are hard to refuse Bob; they never let you go, neither does Peter Blue, whether it's for Queen and Country or his beloved niece Rebecca. If he thinks she is in any danger he won't hesitate to call in old favours.'

'Is that Daniel Manning's story?'

'Possibly, but he remains dutifully employed by the Service too.'

'But he also works for Peter and he retired from the Security Services years ago?'

'As I said, the Service never lets one go and Peter won't hesitate to use whatever it takes, including past and present operatives. You should know that from the Cambridge fiasco.'

'Was it Daniel who did for Albert Brock? If so he must owe Peter too.'

'You could say that.'

'Say what exactly?'

'Sorry Bob, Official Secrets and all that. There is one thing I can tell you about Daniel though; he is very loyal to Peter and you wouldn't want to be on the wrong side of him. I served with him in Bosnia. He was a young operative then.'

'I did get the impression that he's a bit of a loose cannon.'

'Cannon doesn't describe it. Cruise missile might be closer.'

'Did you know he's taken tae sitting outside Spale Investment Company, where Tracey's Harry works?'

'No but I can tell you whatever he is there for it will be for a very good reason. I'm sorry I can't be more help.' He walked to the window. 'Now where's Mark with those buns? Sometimes that lad is beyond me.'

When Mark and Tracey returned from the bakers the four friends sat in the soft chairs normally designated for the use of clients and passed what was left of the afternoon in idle banter.

As they were getting ready to leave Callum asked Bob if he'd care to partake of a dram or two at the Starbank but looked somewhat peeved when his invitation was refused. Bob took hold of his arm and pulled him out of earshot of the others.

It wasn't until Bob and Tracey were on the bridge crossing the river that she asked. 'Well, are ye not going to tell me what that was about?'

'It's not that important.'

'It was important enough that you didnae want me or Mark tae ken what it was. Were ye threatening him?'

'Aye, in a way.'

'About the Molesworth case?'

'No.'

'What then?'

'I was asking if he'd do me the honour of marrying Rebecca and me.'

CHAPTER TWENTY

Thursday 9th July

Bob was out of the house just after seven and parked in George Street well before eight, directly opposite the offices of Spale and Company.

The evening before had not gone well. The atmosphere had turned sour the second Rebecca's taxi pulled onto the driveway and she got out giggling as she paid the driver. Bob merely leaned on the front door frame looking on.

He was expecting an explanation but none came. She squeezed passed him, 'Desperate for the loo.'

He'd resisted the urge to get into his car and drive to Portobello and followed her into the house, slamming the front door as he did so. He waited outside the toilet for her to reappear but when she did she swerved passed him again. 'I could murder a cup of tea.'

Murder wasn't too far from Bob's mind either.

From that moment the evening deteriorated still further and it was only Sophie's return around seven that lightened the atmosphere, if only slightly.

#

From his car he had a full view of Evelyn Spale's offices. It was only then he realised that was exactly where the white van that had run over and killed her husband had been parked. But that was only prior to the hit and run.

He was right in thinking he'd be in position well before Daniel reached his pitch but hadn't given a thought to Harry Cowan. And there he was, quarter to eight and unlocking the large double doors to the office.

Bob had always had a liking for Harry, even though he'd had the pleasure of arresting him on more than one occasion. A likeable rogue was how people thought of him; the type of felon who was always in the process of turning over a new leaf. Thankfully it appeared to be true this time. He began wondering if Jimmy McGuire's salvation was as genuine but his thoughts were interrupted by the tall, bearded figure spreading his blanket on the ground.

As Bob was opening his car door a young female traffic warden appeared. 'Good morning Sir, I hope you're not going to leave this vehicle unattended. Do you realise that you are in a disabled bay? I don't see your disability badge.' She looked around the vehicle.

He stepped from the car and towered over the warden. 'I won't be here long. I just want a word with that gentleman over there.' He pointed to the beggar, the one looking in his direction and smiling broadly.

'Doesn't look your type Sir, if you don't mind my saying?'

Bob took out his police consultant card from his wallet and held it up.

'For a second there I thought you were about to try to bribe me.' She studied the card. 'Consultant, what rank is that?'

'Are you trying to be funny hen?'

'Yes.'

'Pardon?'

'I was trying to be funny.'

He began racking his brain for a suitable reply when Daniel touched him on the shoulder. 'Don't bother Bob, you'll not get the better of Clair.'

'Clair, Clair who? Do you two know each other?'

‘Clair is my minder. She likes keeping an eye on things for me. What is it they say, two heads are better than one and all that.’

‘Bob turned to the warden. ‘Don’t tell me you’re working for the Security Services?’

‘No, I won’t tell you that.’ She touched Daniel on the arm. This gentleman is my employer.’

‘I’ll believe you, thousands wouldn’t,’ replied Bob.

‘Anyway Sir, if you wish a word with my employer you’d better get a move on or you will be required to move your vehicle; there’s a bona fide warden approaching.’ Clair disappeared as quickly as she’d arrived.

‘What an interesting life you lead Daniel.’

‘Mm, you could say that. What can I do for you this fine morning? I take it you know why I’m here?’

‘I do. It’s to do with the tontine. But that’s not why I’m here. I want to talk to you about Charles Molesworth.’

‘What about him, he’s dead isn’t he?’

‘Both he and Willie Dewar. Did you know either of them?’

‘Hardly heard of the former and don’t know the latter. Take it from me, Charles Molesworth’s death has nothing to do with us, if that’s what you are thinking. We’re not all bad you know.’

‘Willie Dewar was linked to Molesworth and died in very suspicious circumstances.’

‘Sorry to disappoint you Bob but I haven’t the faintest idea what you are talking about. I am here because your partner Tod is concerned about Evelyn Spale and JP Associates involvement in recent events to do with Philip Gormand and his somewhat obscure financial practices, that’s all. I’m hoping to help identify those two members of Gormand’s tontine.’

As Daniel was speaking Bob was watching a man walk towards Spale’s and press the intercom. He immediately left Daniel’s side and dashed across George Street. 'Excuse me,' he said to the back of the man's head, 'have we met?'

The second the stranger turned around Bob knew they had.

'I don't think so.'

'In Moffat perhaps, when you were collecting a bag from Philip Gormand? You had a different accent then mind you; Russian, if memory serves me well?'

The man shook his head. 'Listen, whoever you are, I haven't a clue what you are on about and I have business to attend to so would you mind.' He turned his back again.

Bob thought for a moment. 'Goodness, I am sorry, must be old age.'

'Maybe,' answered the man, without turning round again.

Bob walked back across George Street.

'Is that one of the tontine?' asked Daniel.

'Aye,' he answered. 'Now don't you be doing anything daft. Oh, by the way, I meant to ask, how was your trip to Windermere?'

'Oh that, it was lovely. But I think I prefer the Scottish Lochs; they are much colder and deeper and so much more remote.'

#

Bob arrived back in Leith at ten. Tracey wasn't in the office, and neither was Bertie, and he assumed she'd taken him for his morning walk. He called her mobile.

'Bob?'

'Are you taking Bertie for his walk?'

'No, he's at hame. Ma daughter is popping in tae see he's alright.'

'Where are you?'

'Outside Molesworth's.'

'Queen Charlotte Street?'

'No, Jo Molesworth's.'

'Why didn't you tell me?'

'Why didn't you tell me you were gaun to see Daniel Manning?'

'Word travels fast in Leith. What are you doing at Molesworth's wife's?'

'A'm waiting for the boyfriend, or whoever he is, coming out.'

'How do you know he's in there?'

'A dinnae.'

'Wait there, I'll be right round.'

By the time he got to the Links, Tracey was walking towards him.

'What happened?' asked Bob.

'I saw him. I think you were right, it might have been the guy in the van, the one whae threatened the laddie who stole Bertie.'

'What in Heaven's name is going on here Tracey!'

'Whatever it is, A dinnae think it's in Heaven's name, dae you?'

'No. But who is this joker?'

'Maybe just her boyfriend?'

'Aye, a boyfriend who spies on folk and threatens young lads and dogs. No, there's more to this than meets the eye.'

'Should we let Jo know what we know?'

'No. What direction did he go in?'

'He walked across the Links and got intae a van very similar tae the one we saw before, then drove towards Queen Charlotte Street.'

'He'd have been cutting through to Constitution Street and then to God knows where.'

'Aye, ye're right there, God will ken.'

Let's take a wander across to Charles's house and see what's what. Oh and Tracey, thanks for doing what you did.'

'Ye mean use my initiative?'

'Aye.'

#

It only took a few minutes to reach Charles Molesworth's house. It was closed and shuttered up and there was no sign of the police presence that had been there constantly over recent weeks.

'Where dae we go fae here boss? Dae ye think we should just wrap the whole thing up? A ken you're worried about Rebecca wie Jo Molesworth. A cannae make head nor tail of any of it. The way it looks is that Molesworth was intae black magic and preying on young girls and it got worse and led tae him murdering them and burying their bodies in his garden. If ye ask me Jo Molesworth is well out of it and might just have escaped wie her life. Whae ever was haunting him must have known what he was really like and they've been the death of him, whether that was Willie Dewar or another of his victims. Nae wonder Molesworth seemed frightened when he came tae see us that morning, he had plenty tae be frightened about.'

'It that your summing up Sherlock?'

'Aye, more or less. We're getting nowhere and we dinnae have the resources tae continue wie the case.'

'So, what about the bloke we've just been following?'

'Dinnae ask me. Maybe he just likes playing high jinks.'

'High jinks? I've not heard that phrase for years.'

'And A've not heard ye mention DI Sandra Laing for days. Have ye seen her recently?'

'No.'

'Maybe it's about time ye did. Why don't we go tae see her now? Maybe she could help us make a decision on the case.'

'Good idea.'

They began walking back across the Links.

'By the way, Tod's writing a book,' Tracey commented.

'Pardon?'

‘A saw Tod last night, he’s writing that book he’d thought about writing years ago, Lullaby of the Soul A think he’s calling it.’

‘About bloody time; he’s been banging on about that for years. Bob was taking his phone from his jacket pocket to phone Sandra when Tracey grabbed his arm.

‘Look at that.’

‘What?’

‘It’s the black van.’

The van was parked on the north west corner of the Links, by the tennis courts, barely fifty metres from where they stood. ‘Nip across and get me the reg, I’ll be waiting outside the cop shop. They’re owe me a favour or three.’

When she returned with the registration Bob was already standing at reception. ‘Oh Diane, this is Tracey my secre…partner.’

‘Pleased to meet you Tracey. Is it business partner or more intimate than that?’

‘Business partner,’ answered Tracey, somewhat indignantly.

‘I did think you were a wee bit young for DI James.’

‘Right girls, if we can dispense with the comedy and cut to the chase. Bob was remembering the night outside this station when he’d implied to a young constable that he was having a clandestine relationship with his secretary. ‘Diane, would you mind checking this reg number for me please.’ He handed her the slip of paper.

Diane typed the number into the computer and waited only a few seconds. ‘Interesting.’

‘What?’

‘It belongs to a Ford van registered to an undertaker business situated near your office on Great Junction Street.’

‘Not Dunstanes?’ asked Bob.

‘The very one.’

‘Thanks Diane, I’m owe you one.’ Bob turned to go.

‘I’ll add it to the list Inspector.’

They stopped outside the door of the station. ‘If he works at Dunstanes, why is his van parked here?’ asked Tracey.’

‘Free parking?’

‘There’s free parking much nearer than this at the Banana Flats.’

‘Maybe he’s trying to get fit, but he could have walked from Jo’s to his work if that was the case, it’s about the same distance.’

Why don’t we go and ask him in person?’

‘Good idea.’

#

They were at the undertakers in no time. Bob held the door for Tracey then led the way in.

‘Yes, can I help you?’ asked a small, delicate man in his late fifties.

‘Hello. This is my niece Wilma. She has recently lost her husband and I am helping her with the funeral arrangements.’ Bob stretched out his hand. ‘John Roberts. You were recommended to us.’

‘We do have a reputation for excellent service. Can I ask who recommended you?’ It was a friend of Wilma’s husband. He mentioned one particular member of staff; I can’t remember the name but he said he was very tall and slim. He was so impressed by him.’

‘That will be our Raymond. I’m sorry but he’s not here at the moment.’

‘Of course, you must be very busy. We can call back. It would be nice for my niece to have a staff member who’d been recommended by her husband’s friend.’

‘Oh of course I understand but unfortunately Raymond is not at work. He’s been having some family difficulties recently and has taken family care leave. ‘He may be off some time.’

'That's okay, we can wait.'

'But what about your husband's body?'

At that, both investigators left the shop.

#

It was around this same time that Tod, in the middle of lunch, stood from the trestle table and stepped over the bench seat.

'Where're ye gaun Son?' asked Jimmy McGuire. Jimmy always sat next to Tod at mealtimes. Tod was well aware he was under Jimmy's protection, as well as that of his other eleven literacy learners who insisted on sharing the same crowded table.

'I've just remembered I've an important phone call to make.'

'Can A ask who?'

'It was something Tracey told me last night, I thought I'd follow it up.'

Oh well, if it's something tae dae wie Tracey ye'd better use this.' Jimmy took a brand-new mobile phone from his overalls pocket and handed it to him. 'Ye dinnae want the wardens nebbing in on the public phone now, dae ye.'

Once in his cell he closed the door and dialed the number.

'Yes?'

'Val, it's me, Tod.'

'Another new phone eh?'

Tod laughed. 'Compliments of you know who. It's a cellphone.'

'Very funny. Jimmy's God is certainly benevolent.'

'He is that.'

'Isn't this your lunchtime?'

'I wanted to ask you something.'

'Must be important for you to miss lunch Dougal.' Valerie always used her pet name for him when she knew he was up to something. But even she with her wily ways couldn't see what was coming.

'Will you marry me?'

Silence.

'Are you still there?'

'I am.'

'Well, will you?'

'Let me check my diary. I've quite a schedule at the moment.'

'Valerie?'

'Yes.'

'Pardon?'

'Yes, I said. Did Tracey tell you that Bob and Rebecca are going to tie the knot?'

The silence at the other end of the phone was Tod contemplating a benevolent lie but he held it back. 'She did say something about it last night.' He tried to sound vague.

'What a coincidence, don't you think?'

'I never really thought about it.'

'Would you like me to ask Callum if he could do the necessary?'

'That's a good idea.'

'He's marrying our friends.'

'Really. That is a coincidence.'

'You'd better get back to your lunch before it gets cold Dougal.'

Tod put the phone back in his pocket and strode purposefully back to the dining area and handed it back to Jimmy.

'Just keep it Son, they're ten a penny about here.'

'Thanks.'

'What did she say?'

'Who?'

'Valerie.'

'Have you got a listening device in this thing?' Tod held up the phone.

‘No, Tracey told me last night that she’d told you about Bob and Rebecca and we took bets that you’d be next. Mind you, we never thought it would be this quick.’

‘Am I that easily read?’

‘Two peas in a pod you and Bob James, two peas in a pod.’

#

Having had Bob point out one of the remaining members of Gormand’s tontine, Daniel hoped it wouldn’t be too long before the other turned up too.

His hope had proved right and within an hour of Bob leaving, another slightly older very confident looking gentleman was entering the premises of Spale Investment Company. It was another two hours before the two men left, seen to the door by a distraught Evelyn Spale.

That told Daniel all he needed to know. He lifted his blanket from the pavement and beckoned his assistant over. ‘I’m getting too old for this Clair.’

‘Quite possibly Sir.’

‘You didn’t have to agree. Did you message Sean with a description?’

‘Yes Sir.’

‘He should be in the Land Rover on Hanover Street, that’s the direction the oligarchs are heading. With a bit of luck they’ll take the zebra crossing to continue their way along George Street.

It was only another minute before they heard the loud bang and screams coming from the corner of George Street and Hanover Street. Daniel and Clair walked across George Street and climbed into a small Mercedes city car. ‘You’ll have to ask the office for a bigger car Clair.’

‘I’ll have to get further up the pecking order before that. And I couldn’t possibly tell them it was you who suggested it. I’m not supposed to be here remember. Now, where to Sir?’

‘Silly me, neither you are. Take a right, I want to see the damage then I think brunch to be in order, don’t you?’

‘An excellent idea Sir.’

As they passed the junction they saw no sign of the Land Rover but they could see the two men lying crushed on the crossing and a growing crowd scurrying around them. Then they heard the sirens.

‘May I congratulate you on a job well done Sir?’

‘You may Clair and you may agree with me that it is somewhat of a coincidence when one thinks of that Ptolemy Spale met a similar end almost on the same spot.’

‘It most certainly was.’

CHAPTER TWENTY-ONE

Friday 10th July

Bob and Tracey had arranged to visit Sandra in Portobello at eleven. They were armed with croissants.

'You've certainly come up in the world Bob James. I thought doughnuts were more you cup of tea?' Sandra was filling the kettle. 'Did you hear about the accident in Hanover Street yesterday? It was really awful. Two middle-aged Russians it would seem from their identity cards. It's lucky there was no-one else on the crossing or it could have been mayhem.

'It's not long since Ptolemy Spale was killed in the same way just around the corner from there. The Land Rover involved in yesterday's accident didn't stop and from the description it is very like the one that ran over and killed the bloke outside Philip Gormand's in Murrayfield earlier in the year.

'Aye, that's what I was thinking,' replied Bob. 'Do you think it might be some rogue ex-soldier on the warpath. Either that or something involving the Russian Secret Service?'

'Mm.'

'There might have been bairns on that crossing,' added Tracey.

It wouldn't have happened had there been, thought Bob, it might have happened at Loch Lomond instead.

'What's happening at Spale and Company since Philip Gormand's demise?' asked Sandra suddenly.

She was always a mind-reader thought Bob. 'No idea.'

Liar, thought Tracey. 'My Harry's getting on well there, he's been promoted to office manager.'

'She's a good woman, Evelyn Spale and an intelligent one too. If she promoted Harry it's because of his ability.'

'Aye,' said Tracey, still thinking otherwise.

Once the coffee was made they sat down at the table.

'Do these need heating?' asked Sandra, lifting the bag of croissants.

'Aye, better stick them in the oven for five, though they were fresh yesterday.

'Yesterday! And I was thinking I'm special.' She put them in the oven.

'Talking about heating, how is my old boiler?'

'I'm fine thanks, though still waiting for the results of the biopsies.' She joined them again. 'How are you sleuths coping without your main woman and resident DI?'

'Not bad,' answered Tracey.

'Mm,' answered Bob.

'Has the Chief Inspector contacted you yet?'

'No. Why should he?'

'Margaret Whalen has put in a complaint against you and JP Associates.'

'So what's new? We were never flavour of the month with Margaret. What's she bumping her gums about now?'

'You were at Willie Dewar's when he was found dead and it's looking like he was killed in suspicious circumstances.'

'And she thinks that we did it! That's a laugh,' said Bob.

'No, not that. But it is their case. You shouldn't have been there!'

'If you remember correctly Sandra, it was you who took us on board with the Molesworth case.'

'Wrong. I asked if you would come with me to Molesworth's after he was found dead. I did not ask JP Associates for help.'

'I still don't understand what all the fuss is about. Oh by the way, the croissants smell done.'

'Tracey, would you mind getting them from the oven; Bob and I have to clarify a few points here.'

When DI Laing used that tone, it was time to duck, thought Bob.

'Margaret's complaint is not only that you might be a murderer, though you might be about to be murdered. It was you who discovered Charles Molesworth's body in the early hours of the morning in Queen Charlotte Street. Both you and Tracey.

Tracey dropped the tray of croissants but didn't move.

'Sandra…'

'No, don't bother Bob. I can't believe that you'd do this to me, especially now.'

'I can explain.'

'It's not me you'll have to explain to, it's the boss, the lawmakers, the press and every other bloody party bent on destroying our reputation. What in Heaven's name came over you? Falsifying evidence, perverting the course of justice. Have you lost your marbles completely?'

'It was my fault,' interrupted Tracey, putting the croissants back on the tray.

'I don't think so Tracey, and you'll get no brownie points for defending your boss. There's a baking brush in the drawer by the sink if you want to wipe these down – luckily I washed the floor this morning.'

'It was me,' Tracey repeated. 'Bob didn't want to go there that night because he didn't want the ridicule of people finding out that the great DI had been chasing ghosts but I insisted. I'd promised our client, Charles Molesworth, that we would be there.'

'What in Heaven's name for?'

‘It wisnae in the name of Heaven, that’s for sure. Hell would be mair appropriate. He’d come tae us that morning begging for help. He thought he was being haunted.’

‘How did Margaret find out?’ interrupted Bob.

‘Remember the young constable you met outside the police station prior to going to Molesworth’s?’

‘Aye.’

‘Walter you said his name was when we visited Molesworth’s; the son of your second-cousin was how you put it.’

‘Sorry Sandra.’

‘No, he is not your second-cousin, but he does have a cousin and she goes by the name of Margaret Whalen. She has known about your involvement in this case from the moment you told him you were meeting your secretary. He followed you along the street you big glaik!’

‘What a bastard.’

‘We go back a long way Bob. Why did you not tell me what had happened?’

‘We really are sorry Sandra.’

‘You can forget the “we” for starters. Tracey has nothing to do with this and remember that. In fact, neither do you now.’

‘I don’t understand?’

‘I’ve had a word with the Chief Inspector. Walter didn’t see Tracey that morning for one thing. He didn’t actually see you enter Molesworth’s house either. That was all supposition. In fact, he made that bit up under instruction from Margaret. Turns out the Chief already knew that she had it in for you; she’d made that abundantly clear when in the canteen and word travels fast and far in Fettes, as you know. She liked to share her dislike of you with all and sundry. I explained to the Chief what she’d been up to regarding tarnishing your reputation and how she plotted to destroy my career as well, particularly after our relationship ended. What Margaret didn't know though was that Sammy Brogue and I are old pals and he didn't hesitate to back up my story and sign my statement.'

'Good old Sammy.'

'What about good old Sandra?'

'Mm, you could have told me the last part first. What will happen now?'

Sandra smiled for the first time that morning. 'Unfortunately Margaret has been asked to leave the service. Her cousin has been given a very severe warning and has retracted his witness statement.'

'Sandra, seriously, how can I repay you?'

'Bring fresh croissants next time.'

'I was thinking more in the realms of a kiss.'

'No, you're fine but thanks all the same.' Sandra thought for a moment. 'Why did you leave Molesworth's in such a hurry that night Bob? It's really not like you. It must be more than fear of ridicule; there's no way on this earth you would allow ridicule to tarnish your reputation.'

'He's feird of ghosts,' interrupted Tracey.

'What?' asked Sandra incredulously.

'Who told you that?' asked Bob, looking hard at Tracey. 'No, don't bother, I think I know the answer.'

'Tod was worried that your phobia would affect your work on the case so he told me tae watch out for ye.'

'So the great Detective Inspector Bob James is feird of ghosts,' laughed Sandra. 'I thought with the amount of spirits you'd put away in your life you'd be immune.'

'Very funny. It's a private matter, alright!'

'Not when it affects your work, then it affects everyone around you.' Sandra decided to do him the favour of changing the subject, slightly. 'So where does that leave us? Do we hire Ghost Busters or are we going to solve this case on our own?'

'You're supposed to be taking a back seat remember,' replied Bob.

'Oh aye, so I am. Well maybe solving this will help take my mind of other, more pressing problems.' She held her hand to her breast.

After Tracey refilled the kettle the two investigators brought Sandra up to speed with the case, including their tracking down of the undertaker and the visit to the business which employs him.

'They're obviously an item,' added Tracey as an afterthought.

Bob reached for a cold croissant. 'Where the hell could he have disappeared to so quickly when he left his van yesterday morning?'

'He could have gone anywhere,' answered Sandra; there are lanes and alleys around that whole area and it's only a few minutes' walk from the Links to the bus stops which service a multitude of Lothian's finest going in all directions.'

'No, I don't wear that,' said Bob. 'He's got to be somewhere local.'

Sandra thought for a moment. 'What about the Fishermens Union office, it's only just along the road in Constitution Street. Why don't you give that a go first?'

Bob knew that the Fishermens Union office had been boarded up since the death of Willie Dewar but Sandra had just given him his get-out clause. 'That's a good idea. Come on Sherlock, we'll give that a try and see what's what.'

'Would you like me to come with you?' asked Sandra.'

'No, that definitely would not be a good idea. It's too near the cop shop for a start and you can't be seen to be working, especially with JP Associates. We'll check it out and get back to you. I'll pop along tomorrow, there's something of a more social nature I want to run past you.'

'How intriguing. Do you know what that is Tracey?'

'Aye, A think I do but my lips have been well and truly sealed.'

'Double intrigue.' The Detective Inspector stood and lifted the empty tray. 'Well you made short work of yesterday's croissants. Now you'd better get on your way before it gets dark, one never knows what's afoot in the witching hours.'

#

There's no way Dr Death is going to be in the Fishermens Union office,' said Bob as they got to the car.

'I agree.'

'I've got to admit Tracey, I'm still completely flummoxed.'

'Me tae, but never thought I'd hear you saying it. I never thought I'd here masel saying this either, but there's only one person who can find out what this joker is up tae.'

'Who?'

'Harry Cowan.'

CHAPTER TWENTY-TWO

Saturday 11th July

It was nearing eight when Harry parked his van almost directly outside Jo Molesworth's house. He'd hardly had time to pull on the handbrake when the man he'd seen on Jo's door-cam appeared. He was walking towards the house and had a newspaper under one arm and carried what Harry took to be a bag of rolls. Although the man was obviously an early riser, he looked sleepy.

Harry leaned back against the seat of the van and thought about his last stake-out for JP Associates. That was in Murrayfield Road and if it hadn't been for that vagrant, the one who'd taken to sitting outside Spale's, he may not have lasted the night. That thought sent a shiver up his spine, causing him to look left and right across a misty Leith Links. Letting out a sigh he began settling in for his shift.

#

Just as he was doing so the Reverend Callum Mackie was unlocking the door to BEYOND. He too was an early riser but never usually this early, especially on a Saturday. But he'd been summoned here to meet Daniella. Her shift at the local Chemists started at nine and she wanted to run something by him, or that's what she'd said when she telephoned the night before.

He'd just filled the kettle when the intercom buzzed. 'Good morning Callum, I hope I haven't got you from your bed too early.'

He pressed the door release without replying.

Daniella walked swiftly into his office and put a round, flat cake on his desk. He didn't think he'd seen one like it nor anyone wearing such vibrantly coloured clothes. 'Is that cake for me?'

'Of course it's for you, and me, my mother's recipe, straight out of Africa. I hope you like dates.'

'He was just thinking that this was one date he could do without. 'How lovely. Do you wish a coffee? Or tea?'

'Coffee would be very nice.'

He had his back to her and was filling the coffee machine. 'So, what is so urgent that you need to speak to me at the weekend?'

'Time and tide waits for no man. You should know that more than anyone, being an old seadog. It's about your charity.'

'I see you've done your research on me Daniella, but I think that Dr le Mot and I have BEYOND in hand.'

'I believe you do, but surely you'll not refuse a pharmacist willing to work for you part-time and for free?'

He turned, coffees in hand. 'Pardon?'

'You'd have made a good barista, those look wonderful. I was thinking that as I'm dishing out methadone at the chemists and getting to know the users while doing so, we could have a ready-made client group.'

He sat down and sipped his coffee. 'Mm. It's our new coffee machine, Mark insisted. I thought you weren't convinced by BEYOND? That's how it seemed to Mark and me.'

'I'm not, but instinct tells me that you are the right people to help those with addictions to find another path, or should I say a path other than methadone, and I want to help. You obviously have much life experience and Mark will be a good counsellor one day. She reached out her hand to shake his before he could answer. Now are we going to eat Mum's cake before that lovely coffee gets cold? I was sure you'd have a knife to cut it.'

He looked at the cake while pondering on her being sure he'd have a knife. In the Special Boat Service he'd build quite a reputation for being handy with a knife.

'Did you say something Callum?'

'No. I was just going to welcome you aboard.' For some reason Daniella's name suddenly reminded him of its male counterpart, Daniel.

'Aboard, that's a very good metaphor I must say, for a project by a river, run by a man who spent much of his life at sea.'

'How do you know about…no don't bother to answer that.' He held up his cup; 'Cheers.'

#

Bob had not raised the subject of Jo Molesworth with Rebecca again, hoping that his own investigation would bear fruit well before she got herself in too deep. This did not stop her from brooding on the subject.

'Bobby, if you can stop thinking about the elephant in the room for a moment, did you notice if I've left my iPad on the couch?'

Bob ignored her. 'I see that Sophie was out again last night.'

'She's a big girl and can go out on her own,' answered Rebecca.

'But she didn't come home till after one.'

'It seems that you are extremely protective of both girls in this house. Perhaps over-protective at times, though far be it from me to think that.'

He lifted the Weekend Telegraph from the stool beside his chair. 'I see that the Tory MPs are still rambling on about nothing in particular and making a few bob into the bargain.'

She brought his coffee over to him. 'Would you like me to order the Sun? I believe they still do a page 3 girly.'

He put the coffee on the stool and grabbed hold of her arm and pulled her onto his knee. 'Now why would I want a page 3 girl when I have you?'

She tried to wriggle free. 'Let me go you big brute.'

'What are you up to today?'

'Why? I thought I might do a spot of gardening.'

'It's about time.'

'What?'

'Timing, I meant. Could you spare the morning?'

'Why?'

'I've made an appointment at Hamilton and Inches. You do want a ring, do you not?'

#

Harry was getting peckish by eleven and was about to risk leaving the stake-out for a trip to Greggs when Jo's door opened and she and her companion appeared. She was dressed casually in tight pants and a dark sweater. He was wearing black jeans and a black shirt. Quite fitting for an undertaker, thought Harry, immediately regretting that he'd not brought a sandwich, as Tracey had suggested.

When the pair crossed the road and skimmed passed the back of his van his worst fears were realised. They were walking to wherever they were going.

He watched them cross the Links and was about to get out of the van and follow them on foot then changed his mind and began texting. **'Hacker, could you hone in on the Links? A couple, both wearing black, heading towards Queen Charlotte Street. I'm following in my van.'**

He waited a few seconds. 'Yer no allowed a van on the Links.'

'Very funny!'

'Stay on your phone. I'll give a running commentary.'

Harry started his van and drove down Links Garden towards Queen Charlotte Street.

'They're at the tennis courts.'

'I'm almost there.'

‘Maybe gaun for a game?’

‘Concentrate Hacker!’

‘They’ve crossed the road onto Queen Charlotte Street.’

‘I’ll stop here. A dinnae want them tae see me.’

‘Shit.’

‘Yer no needing the loo?’

‘No, numpty. You’ll no believe where they’ve just gaun.’

‘Where? Intae Molesworth’s house?’

‘No, the house next door.’

‘Help ma boab. Thanks Hacker, A mean it.’

‘Nae bother Harry, anytime.

Harry immediately telephoned Tracey, who immediately telephoned Bob, who immediately telephoned Sandra, who agreed that it would be a nice gesture to give DI Sammy Brogue the opportunity of finding out exactly what was going on. She gave Bob the honour of phoning him.

If Sammy Brogue considered it an honour to have the pleasure of arresting Jo Molesworth, he certainly did not get any pleasure from what they found in the premises next door to the lawyer’s, nor from having to work a double shift at the weekend.

As his new DS put it, they’d have found no worse in Beelzebub’s lair. In the attic room there was an assortment of artifacts that could only have been related to occult practices. A skeleton and skulls, masks, goat’s head, complete with horns, jewelled goblet to name but a few. Two robes hung on the attic door – one white, one black and each had a hood similar to that of medieval monks.

When they found the hidden door to the lawyer’s attic they saw the pentagram drawn on the floor.

But it wasn’t what they found in both attics that shocked them the most. While Jo Molesworth and her partner looked on, the police team moved meticulously through the house till they reached the cellars.

DI Brogue led the way through the small door. The first thing the others heard after he entered was the sound of retching. His DS immediately rushed through the door to find his boss with his hand against the wall leaning hard. Before the constable could ask what was wrong he glanced to the centre of the cellar. On trestles, and in coffins, lay the bodies of three young girls, each in differing stages of decomposition.

#

It was very soon after that discovery that Sammy got the pleasure of making the arrests. Once in Constitution Street police station interview rooms Jo Molesworth began her defence by blaming Raymond Cox, her accomplice, for the whole thing. She wove a tale about him being a practicing wizard who had taken her under his spell. They'd met three years before when she was still in counselling. Raymond had come up with the idea of putting Charles out of her life and mind forever and planned the whole thing. Jo could barely communicate this through her tears of anguish.

But that wasn't the story that was being told in the interview room next door. Raymond had never married and lived with his ailing mother when he met Jo, or as he put it, fell in love with her. He'd never had a girlfriend, which didn't surprise the interview team as it appeared he had a difficulty focussing on what they were saying and very obviously had a personal hygiene problem.

When one of the detectives suggested that Charles had been a very bad man and that was why his wife was trying to destroy him, Raymond replied that he'd spoken with Charles just after meeting Jo and that he was a very kind man. Charles had given him money for his Mum to get a carer and even visited her. Once, when he was in Charles's office, the lawyer showed him photographs and letters he'd been sent from the family of the girl who'd died in the Hague. He'd been sending money to the family ever since their daughter had died. The photographs and letter were kept with his bank transfer receipts in an album which he kept in a safe in his office. He said he was the only one with a key and when Jo tried to get it, she couldn't find it. It was just after that she decided the only way to get that key was to get rid of Charles and she came up with the plan.

#

It took all of what was left of that day and the Sunday for Jo Molesworth and her partner to admit to their crimes in full. The house they'd used was owned by Jo and had been given to her by her husband, who'd bought it as a job lot with his own house. Apparently, though agreeing to the separation, he still wanted her nearby.

The only murder she and her accomplice had committed, according to Jo, was that of her husband Charles, who had been quite literally scared to death. The bodies of the young girls, like those that had been discovered in Charles's garden, had been removed from the crematorium prior to cremation, over a period of two years. The girls targeted by the undertaker had all been homeless with no next of kin and had been taken by Jo's partner for burial in Molesworth's garden; the purpose being to have him accused of murder, should their plans to scare him to death fail.

Once it had dawned on Jo Molesworth that it was pointless continuing with the lies, her demeanor changed and she turned from fraught widow into a malignant force, admitting proudly the whole affair. She almost spat out that from the time she'd set eyes on her ill husband she'd seen her opportunity. She still remained resentful that the powers that be had removed her from the hospital where Charles was but she was never going to give up, even if that meant burning down the house of the doctor who'd barred her from the hospital. It was easy enough to scare Charles as he had never totally recovered from the death of the young girl in the Hague.

Towards the end of the interview she admitted that none of her story about her husband and young girls was true. She seemed to find this part hilarious and laughed out loud at the thought. According to her, he wasn't the least bit interested in sex.

Asked if she had any regrets regarding what she'd done her only comment was, 'I should have done it years ago.'

#

As he walked alone from the police station DI Brogue was pondering on his lost weekend. The post-mortem results on Willie Dewar had arrived at Fettes at mid-day on the Saturday and been emailed across to Queen Charlotte Street. Sammy couldn't get over the result of the post-mortem and wasn't sure he really believed it. According to forensics Dewar had died from legionnaires' disease that he'd contracted when he opened the new bag of compost he was using in his garden. Their story was that about **1 out of 10 people who get the disease, die from legionella infection. The bacteria itself can lie dormant in compost contained in plastic sacks.**

He was just thinking that he might look into that further when he heard the shout.

'You look like you could murder a pint Sammy.' It was Bob, and Sandra.

'I could murder something, that's for sure!'

CHAPTER TWENTY-THREE

Saturday 22nd August

Most of the organising for the double wedding had been left to Tracey Cowan who had chosen as Rebecca's best maid. She in turn asked the Reverend Callum Mackie for his help and guidance.

Tod's best-man had offered to help but as he was behind bars that could have made things quite difficult, especially when he told Tod that he still had friends on the outside who could arrange everything for cash. Jimmy did insist however that if he was to be best man it would have to be a church service. 'A've never been in a church Tod,' he'd said, 'A found ma God in here. So A want tae be in one now, it might be ma last chance.'

'It wasn't too difficult to arrange with the Prison Management to give special dispensation for them to be released for the day, wardens in tow of course.

What Jimmy was able to arrange from behind bars was for Tod to be fitted with an exquisite three-piece suit, compliments of an old tailor who, like Jimmy, had spent more years behind bars than one could shake a stick at.

He also made sure that Tod was able to choose a wedding ring for Valerie. The tray of rings was brought in specially by the brother of another inmate. Tod didn't ask which Jewellers the brother owned nor why the price for such a wedding ring was so cheap.

The only problem which arose was that once Tod had chosen the ring and explained to Jimmy that he, as best man, would be the one to present it to him during the ceremony. Jimmy broke into tears at which was not what Tod had expected. When Jimmy looked up he only asked that Tod never mention those tears.

For all his freedom, Callum's job was anything but easy. Since the decision to have a double wedding he'd been working hard with the elders from his previous parish kirk to get agreement on holding the wedding there. Meeting after meeting, phone-call after phone-call, email after email yet he couldn't budge the elders. Convicts and their wardens at a ceremony in their church! The other big question was whether any of the betrothed were practising Christians? Even the presbytery were called in to a special meeting where Callum tried to convince that traditions could be eased for one afternoon. Deaf ears was what he was thinking to himself on the evening in question. In the end he'd given up and handed it over to Tracey who in turn asked her preacher in the Baptist Church if they could use his church, to which he replied an immediate yes, with no questions asked.

The Pastor apologised that the church hall was not big enough to host the celebrations afterwards and he knew they'd understand that alcohol was a "no no" in his church. This caused discussion, instigated by Bob, about where the wedding celebration would take place.

Beccy offered her place as it was big enough, but everyone agreed that wouldn't be right. Bob suggested Mal Maison but Valerie thought the Bowling Club where they'd met with Big Jake just before he died more appropriate. Sandra, who'd received news from the Maggie Centre that her tumour was benign, agreed with Valerie, but then she would, said Rebecca, as she was to be Valerie's best maid.

Sophie couldn't see the problem of having the do in the bowling club either but her Mum quickly put her right on that score; the job of a maid of honour was to agree with the bride, or else!

It was Evelyn Spale who saved the day by suggesting that she bear the full cost of the reception and hire a marquee to be erected in her garden. Evelyn had brightened up recently and everyone put that down to her beginning to recover from the death of her husband Ptolemy. Not wanting to stall her recovery in any way they all agreed that hers was the best idea; well everyone bar the prison authorities, who deemed it not secure enough. The question then arose as to how the prisoners could be prevented from escaping between the tent pegs. It was only when Evelyn agreed to install close circuit cameras with a direct link to the Governor's office that he was persuaded to allow his charges to attend.

Harry took responsibility for arranging the transport. Both brides would be brought from their homes to the church in a shared wedding car. Bob and Harry would make their way by taxi though it was a black maria, or sweat box, that would be delivering Tod and his best man Jimmy McGuire.

An open-topped double-decker bus would be transporting everyone, bar Tod and Jimmy, from the church to Evelyn's house. This left them all somewhat nervous and checking the weather forecast for Edinburgh for the 22nd August. As it turned out there was no need to worry, the sun shone from morning till night on the day, causing Harry, never one for religion, to look to Heaven and cross himself more than once.

#

The man who would be giving Rebecca away, her Uncle Peter, surprised everyone by turning up in full Highland dress. He'd tried to talk his driver Sean into doing the same but he insisted that an Irishman would not be seen dead in such a thing. Sean had not been himself recently and Peter merely put that down to the young man's regret that he had not yet found a bride. The unusual thing was that for some unknown reason, Sean had taken to watching the Scottish news intently each day and buying up every newspaper title in their local newsagents. Peter said nothing about this and left him more or less to his own strange devices.

#

Tracey and Harry stood on the front steps of the church and watched as a dark grey saloon car drew up opposite and two men and a woman got out. 'Plain clothed polis if ever A've seen them,' said Harry.

'A ken one of them,' replied Tracey.

'Ye do?' Which one?'

'The one in front is DI Sammy Brogue. He came tae the scene of Willie Dewar's death when Bob and A were there.'

'What are they wanting here?'

'Dinnae ask me.'

The Detective Inspector walked up to them. 'Good afternoon Tracey, lovely day for a wedding.'

'What are you daen here, everything is ligit?'

'We're invited.'

'Bob never said.' She looked across at the other two. 'Are they invited tae?'

'Yep. Never go anywhere without my heavy team.'

She was about to enquire further when Bob appeared. 'Afternoon Sammy, I see you've brought Mary and your new partner.'

'Aye, still a cadet and not completed his probation but he's got the makings of a good polisman.'

'I'm sure. Sergeant Sandy Waterstone wouldn't have it any other way. You could get him running the station sweepstake too; he's a whizz kid with figures.'

'So I've heard.'

Tracey couldn't believe her ears, nor her eyes. She focussed in on the male policeman and immediately rushed across the street. 'Josh!'

‘Hi Tracey, my Dad thought it would be a good idea. I’m sorry I can’t take up the offer of a job with JP Associates. I’m on my probationary period and Detective Inspector Brogue thought this would be good experience.’

Aye, thought Tracey, and Detective Inspector Brogue has a sense of humour too. ‘A’m so glad you’re here; it’s great tae see ye.’

She walked back across the street to join Bob and the detective just in time to hear the conversation. ‘No such thing as a free midnight pint, eh Bob.’

‘The prison authorities asked if we could have a police presence. Evelyn Spale is putting on the do in her garden and they were worried Tod and Jimmy might escape. It should be a good do. Greggs are doing the buffet. Tom Kitchin’s doing the meal.’

‘Some good news at last,’ said the DI returning to his team.

‘You are a wily one Bob James, so ye are.’

As Tracey said this, Evelyn approached. ‘We’ve got a wee problem; the church pastor has just brought it to my attention.’

‘What is it?’

‘I’ve asked your Harry if he can help.’

‘What wie?’

She walked around Tracey and pointed along the pavement. Sitting no more than ten yards from the entrance to the church was a beggar. ‘I’ve seen him before. He was sitting outside our office the day those men were killed in that hit and run. Harry tried to move him along but he wouldn’t go. What a coincidence that he’s here today.’

Aye, so it is thought Tracey. ‘Maybe this is his usual patch. He might only come up town on high days and holidays. Where is Harry?’

‘I’m not sure, I think he’s maybe a little wary of the man.’

‘He’s a big bloke.’

They were still looking at the apparition when the black prison van stopped right outside the church. Tod and Jimmy were escorted from the rear of the vehicle. Each one had two uniformed prison officers. Jimmy immediately spotted the beggar. 'What's he daen here?'

'Leave him to me Jimmy,' said Tod.

'He's not gaun tae spoil your day. Get him out of here, or A will.'

Tod asked his escort if they would escort him to the man. They agreed but kept the handcuffs on.

Bob watched Tod and his guards approach Daniel and pulled Evelyn off to the side, away from Tracey, and told her all about the man.

#

'Good afternoon Daniel. May I congratulate you in person on a job well done.'

'Thank you kind Sir. Thanks to Harry and Hacker, all the monies from the tontine are now Proceeds of Crime and just maybe some of it has reached the right hands. Mrs Spale has put Harry and Hacker Hanson forward as the people who solved the crime and the Government is giving them a very substantial reward of five percent of all proceeds. When you consider there was more than one hundred million pounds in that account, five percent is not a bad shout.'

'Harry's not told Tracey yet.' Tod looked around at the gathering. 'I take it you weren't officially invited to the wedding?'

'I'm invisible remember. Peter Blue prefers it that way.'

'Oh yes, I forgot.' Tod sat down, pulling the warden with him. 'You'll see Valerie.'

Daniel didn't answer.

'I am sorry.'

‘It’s me who’s sorry Tod. That’s what one gets when one puts the Service first.’

‘Is there anything I can do?’

‘What, a last-minute invitation? Just make sure she has a fabulous day and a good life.’

‘Are you going to remain here?’

‘She won’t recognise me. Anyway, who else is going to look after your lot? Certainly not that motley crew that got out of the car across the street.

‘Very true,’ said Tod, looking back at the police.

The beggar smiled, lifted his hat from the pavement and held it out to the wardens. ‘Penny for your thoughts kind Sirs.’

The wardens stood and pulled at Tod. ‘I don’t know what it is that you are involved in Tod, but I’m glad it’s not my problem.’

#

BEYOND’s new assistant Daniella was invited to be Callum’s personal assistant on the big day. She’d jumped at the chance to get to know Callum and his associates better. But she was left somewhat wide-eyed by the sight of four tall men in black uniforms. At first she took them to be military friends of Callum’s until he explained and apologised for not informing her sooner. That’s when she noticed the handcuffs.

#

When Callum stepped up onto the platform in the church he had full view of the wedding party and couldn’t help but smile. For one, he’d not been in a church in quite some while, and secondly had never been in a Baptist church. But the real reason for the smile was that he’d never witnessed such a varied congregation. God works in mysterious ways he thought as he looked across the gathering.

Bob and Tod sat in the front row with Jimmy McGuire and Harry Cowan and Callum watched as Jimmy wriggled constantly in his chair, fidgeting with his tie and checking his top pocket to make sure Tod's ring was still there.

Harry gripped Bob's wedding ring tightly in his hand and looked as if he was never going to let it go.

Though both Bob and Tod had been married before Callum could see quite clearly that neither of them were immune to wedding day nerves.

It wasn't a big wedding, by Leith standards, but the church was busy enough to create a joyful atmosphere, despite the four wardens who leaned on the side walls and the obvious presence of three plain-clothes police sitting at the rear.

Tracey had asked some of her church family to attend and many of them were there, holding on tightly to their well-worn bibles as they looked around the room. Much of the ceremony had been arranged by Tracey but the wedding party had requested that any religious theme be kept to a minimum. On that news Callum had suggested that they could ask a member of the Humanist Society to take the ceremony. This in turn caused him to be accused of huffiness.

When both brides arrived, only slightly late, the congregation were openly stunned by the beauty of both. Rebecca wore an apple white dress lined with a very narrow strip of green. She carried a bouquet of miniature yellow roses. Valerie wore a pure white dress with no trim and she held a bouquet of small pink flowers. Both women had consciously chosen not to wear low cut garments.

Prior to the betrothal Mark le Mot read from Elizabeth Barret Browning, How do I Love Thee. His occasional glance at Sophie was obvious to many, especially her Great Uncle Peter.

Towards the end the ceremony Callum asked if all could stand for the hymn, How Great Thou Art. This caused Jimmy McGuire to once more break into floods of tears. Gets them every time thought Callum as he wished the couples much joy.

It was after five o'clock when the double-decker bus with the prison van close behind, drew up outside Evelyn's. She'd pulled out all the stops, but before anyone could enter the house the wardens had to check the premises, thoroughly. It was five-thirty before they could make their way through the house to the back garden and the brightly decorated marquee.

Callum stood with Eveyln Spale at the front door of the house welcoming all who had not been at the church. He thought he'd met most of Bob and Tod's acquaintances, until his hand was shaken by a short stocky man with a distinctly Geordie accent. 'Awright Bonnie Lad. Jackie Gould to you, this is the wife, Nan.'

Both Callum and Evelyn were still trying to work out who these people were when the next in line stepped forward. 'Alright Minister?'

'And who might you be?' asked Callum with a smile.

'Hacker, Hacker Hanson.'

'I've heard much about you Hacker and am very pleased to meet you in the flesh' said Mrs Spale, shaking his hand. 'Thank you for your assistance with our recent troubles.'

'Nae bother. Thank you for getting us that reward. I'm made up, and so is my mother. I've got her into a brilliant care-home now.'

As he walked away Callum drew her aside. 'What troubles?'

'Oh, it was nothing really. Hacker helped us out with some computer problems.'

The next guest surprised them even more when she announced that she was Tracey's neighbour and had brought Bertie with her. They looked directly behind her for her partner before realising Bertie was Tracey's dog. 'Tracey said Bertie wouldnae miss this for anything.' As if to prove it, Bertie let out a small yelp, before wagging his tail and dashing towards the smell of the buffet.

Callum looked out to see if Bertie was the final guest. 'I think that's it,' he said.'

Eveyln followed his gaze. 'Is that a taxi pulling up on the other side of the road?' I'll go and take a look.' She stepped out through the old wooden porch with its gnarled tree-stump supports and along the path to the gate. An elderly gentleman was being helped from the cab by the driver. They were both laughing loudly. 'Can I help?' she called, as she crossed the road.

'Ah, you'll be Mrs Spale,' said the elderly gentleman. He proffered his right hand to shake hers while holding on to the door of the taxi with the other. 'Tam's been giving me a running commentary about your beautiful city.

'And who might you be?' asked Evelyn.

'Nobody important, just an old retired university Professor.'

'Are you invited to the reception?'

'I believe so. Actually, I was invited to the ceremony but thought that it might be over-taxing so decided to remain in my hotel.'

'Who invited you?'

'The groom, or one of them. Detective Inspector Bob James, not quite retired. If you don't mind you can tell him Professor Kirkland from Cambridge is here.'

'Professor, I've heard of you.'

'All good I hope?'

'I've heard it said that you were the hero of the day by the River Lark. Well you'd better get yourself in here before they eat all the buffet.' She took his arm and turned towards her cottage. That's when she spotted the beggar sitting not thirty feet away from her house.

#

It turned out that Evelyn wasn't far wrong about the buffet disappearing fast and the only food remaining was a tray of sushi, which looked like it had hardly been touched. The professor left Evelyn's side and wandered over to the table. He chose sticky rice topped with raw cod and seaweed and lifted it to his mouth.

'I wouldn't eat that Professor. I kept these hot for you.' It was Bob and he was holding a plate with sausage rolls and Scots pie cut into bite-size pieces. I had to hide them from the wardens.'

'Well, thank you Bob.' He placed the sticky rice back on its tray. And thank you for the invitation, I'm sorry I couldn't make the ceremony.'

'Never mind that, I'll introduce you. Oh and Professor, keep your hand on the sausage rolls.'

#

After the buffet they took their seats at either side of the three long tables. Both wedding parties were seated at the top table and the guests at the long tables that ran at right angles almost the full-length of the marquee.

Rebecca's Uncle Peter was about to begin his Father of the Bride speech for Rebecca when he realised that Valerie was not yet seated at the table and he couldn't see her in the marquee. 'Ahem, has anyone seen the other bride?'

'She'll not be a minute,' answered Tod, hoping that was the case.

#

'I brought you these.'

'Sushi, how lovely.'

'And this.' She handed him a bottle of malt whisky.

'Thanks, that's more like it.'

'Are you okay Daniel?'

'Fighting fit Val. So, you did recognise me?'

‘I’ve always known. You quite suit the garb, I must say. You know Dan, the way things have turned out, maybe it’s for the best.’

‘I’m sure it is. You wouldn’t want to be married to a beggar now, would you?’

‘Stark choice, beggar or convict.’

‘And an apt choice of words “Stark”, that’s how it all began. There’d be no JP Associates if it hadn’t been for the banker.’

‘Aye. Tod told me everything.’

‘He’s a good man Tod.’

‘I hope so.’

‘He is Val.’

‘Are you still going to keep me under surveillance now that I’m a married woman?’

‘No need. Tod is more than capable of keeping an eye on you.’

‘I’d better be getting back.’

‘Thanks for the sushi, though I must say I’d have preferred one of those sausage rolls.’

‘Don’t tell me you’ve got a video…no, don’t even answer that. Goodbye Daniel, and take care.’

#

The reception went on until three the following morning. Sammy Brogue eventually talked the wardens round into having a drink, all expect the one who’d be driving the van that would take Tod and Jimmy back to jail.

Though a newly married man, Tod had hardly left Tracey’s side, which didn’t bother Valerie one bit at all. She wandered the marquee talking and taking the photographs that would act as sketches for her next painting.

It was in the middle of one of his and Tracey’s conversations that he let the cat out of the bag. ‘So what are you going to do now that you are a rich woman?’

‘A was only Beccy’s best maid; she didnae pay me. And the rise A got fae JP’s doesnae exactly break the bank.’

‘You don’t know yet, do you?’

‘What?’

‘Nothing.’

‘Dinnae gie me “nothing.” Now is not the time for anymore benevolent lies. What is it?’

‘I think you’d better have a word with Harry.’

Nobody bothered counting how many drams Bob had had when he stood, staggered slightly, and declared a toast to one of his best and most loyal friends and associates, Big Jake Robinson. That was the only time the neighbours thought of complaining about the noise.

By 3.30am all was deathly quiet in the marquee. The sun would soon be up and they were all gone, all except Evelyn. She picked up two clean whisky glasses and polished them in turn with a napkin.

Donning her coat she walked to the gate and looked along the street. ‘Mind if I join you Daniel?’ she asked, sitting on the pavement beside him.

He took the bottle from his pocket and poured. ‘It would be my pleasure Mrs Spale.’

THE END

Glossary

Scots – English Translation

A	-	I
aye	-	yes
bam	-	stupid person
beat it	-	go away
cannae	-	can not
cauld	-	cold
clamjamfry	-	a mob, crowd or rabble
clarty	-	dirty
couldnae	-	could not
crabbit	-	bad tempered
cullen skink	-	Scottish Fish Chowder
daen	-	doing
daft	-	stupid person
dinnae	-	do not
eejit	-	stupid person
feart	-	frightened
fish supper	-	fish and chips
gaun	-	go or going
gie	-	give
ginnel	-	small tunnel or stairway
glaikit	-	stupid
gonnae	-	going to
guid	-	good
hadnae	-	had not
havnae	-	have not
hen	-	friendly term for a woman
heid	-	head
intae	-	into
jammy	-	lucky
laddie	-	boy

lintie	-	linnet
ma	-	my
maist	-	most
manky	-	dirty
masel	-	myself
na	-	no
nebbing	-	to pry
nyaff	-	an insignificant person
skint	-	to have no money
thegither	-	together
topped himself	-	committed suicide
whae	-	who
widnae	-	would not
yin	-	one

CPSIA information can be obtained
at www.ICGtesting.com
Printed in the USA
LVHW051127070223
738796LV00015B/1645